Half to Death

By
Robin Alexander

HALF TO DEATH
© 2011 BY ROBIN ALEXANDER

All rights reserved. No part of this book may be reproduced in printed or electronic form without permission. Please do not participate in or encourage piracy of copyrighted materials in violation of the author's rights. Purchase only authorized editions.

ISBN 13: 978-1-935216-31-5

First Printing: 2011

This Trade Paperback Is Published By
Intaglio Publications
Walker, LA USA
WWW.INTAGLIOPUB.COM

This is a work of fiction. Names, characters, places, and incidents are the product of the author's imagination or are used fictitiously, and any resemblance to actual persons, living or dead, businesses, companies, events, or locales is entirely coincidental.

CREDITS

EXECUTIVE EDITOR: TARA YOUNG
COVER DESIGN BY: Tiger Graphics

Dedication

For the sweetest of Roses.

Acknowledgments

I'd like to express my gratitude to the "commanator," Tara Young, who dutifully deletes all my extra commas and makes me look good.

And especially to my love, Becky, who introduced me to Highway 98 and all the towns mentioned in this book. She's extremely patient with me when I want to explore a new strand of beach, and she always helps me carry the pounds of shells I collect.

Prologue

"I see her! Her hoodie's caught on something."

Fear's grip was nearly as cold as the snow and ice Deb lay upon. Her hands, though gloved, felt numb as she held on to Miranda's ankles. The muscles in her stomach and back quivered as she lifted her head to watch the horrifying spectacle unfold. This was all her idea, all her fault.

Last year's resolution was to lose fifty pounds, and she had. While she ran endless miles on a treadmill and stuffed her fingers down her throat after each meal she shouldn't have eaten, she envisioned herself in a form-fitting ski suit. Something that would show off the hard-earned body but wouldn't reveal the stretch marks. But in sunny Florida, no one wore ski suits, so the idea for a winter vacation was born. West Virginia was chosen over Colorado since none of her friends knew how to ski, and no one wanted to humiliate herself in front of thousands as she learned.

Deb supposed that maybe Miranda could share in the blame, too. After all, it was her idea for them to hike into the woods near the cabin. And it was Lonna who wanted to veer off the trail and follow the tracks made by an animal they hoped to glimpse or maybe photograph.

As Deb, the last piece in the four-woman daisy chain, pondered each decision that brought them all to this point, she watched as Lonna struggled to pull Sloan from the breach in the ice. Marty had gone for help, and it seemed like hours had passed since her departure. Deb shivered violently as she wondered how long Sloan had been under the frigid water.

"Let me go," Miranda said as she pulled her boot free of Deb's weak grasp.

"What're you doing?" Deb's teeth chattered so hard she could hardly form the question and bit her tongue in doing so.

Miranda glanced over her shoulder, as she crawled gingerly over the ice. "I'm going to help Lonna. She can't pull Sloan out on her own."

"Are you crazy? We could all go in, and who is going to save us then?" Deb cried as Miranda crawled farther away. Miranda didn't answer, Deb belly-crawled to Angel, the next woman in line, and grabbed her ankles.

The ice groaned and creaked as Miranda and Lonna worked frantically to free their friend. Deb watched as Sloan's dark head came into view and gasped when she looked upon the face—blue, unfamiliar in its pallor, almost inhuman. Lifeless eyes stared past her, and Deb heard the helpless cries of her friends around her. It was her fault, all her fault.

"They're coming! Help is coming!" Marty screamed as she ran as fast as she could through the snow. Tears of relief streamed down Deb's face as a stranger trailed behind her carrying an orange case. Sirens wailed in the distance, but as she gazed back at Sloan's face, she thought it might be all in vain.

Chapter 1

"She's gay. I'd bet my next paycheck on it," Miranda said as we watched the newest trainer at Panacea Workout Center saunter across the room. "She struts like a dyke. Straight women don't carry themselves like that. The nickname cinches it, that's a dyke name."

"Actually, Jade sounds more like a stripper." I'd overheard someone saying she got the nickname because of her eye color, but they looked more emerald to me. "She'd make a lot more money dancing on a pole than trying to whip all of us into shape."

"I bet she's arrogant," Miranda continued, ignoring my comment. "Everyone in here is watching her. She has to know it."

Miranda was right. Along with us, everyone in the room was openly appraising her or sneaking peeks when she thought no one was looking.

"She's taller than half of the men in here. Miranda wiped her face with her towel, her gaze fixed. "She probably thinks she's perfection personified."

"She is." I smiled when Miranda looked my way with a scowl. "Perfect teeth, I saw them once when she half smiled. She doesn't do it often. Flawless skin, no cellulite, beautiful glossy long, dark hair—perfection."

Miranda turned her attention back to the new trainer as Jade demonstrated proper lunge form. "Look at those muscles. She must work her body nonstop. We've been coming here for almost a year, and neither of us looks like that."

"Speak for yourself." I flexed the muscles in my arms. "I've developed some decent guns."

"You have squirt guns in comparison to her, bragapotomus."

"I think you're jealous." I dodged a slap and laughed.

"Of course, I am. I'm married, no lusting allowed, so the only thing I can do is bitch." Miranda shook her head. "You should've seen Marty the other night when we were here. She was staring so hard her feet got tangled on the treadmill. She bounced off the mirror before she even knew what was happening to her."

"Marty came with you? That's a first."

Miranda nodded. "She wanted to have a look at the new girl in town. Some of the people she works with have been talking about her."

"I bet she's lusting with the rest of us," I said with a grin.

"She better not be. If I can't, she can't, either."

I draped my towel around my neck. "Nothing wrong with a couple having a crush on someone as long as they're honest about it and don't take it any further than looking."

"Sloan Hawkins, sometimes you sound like a man." Miranda tossed her towel at me. "Let's get out of here. I promised Marty pizza for dinner. I need to get home so I can negate all the hard work I've done tonight."

"You go ahead." I stood and stretched. "I want to run another mile tonight. I had pizza for lunch."

Miranda shook her head and tsked. "Oh, little player, you're so out of your league with that one. Better leave it alone." She took one last look at Jade and turned to me. "You can tell me all about how she rebuffed you over breakfast in the morning."

I had no intention of making a play for Jade or anyone, but I wasn't going to admit that to Miranda. Nor was I willing to admit that I'd not had a date in over a month. Even a hint of change in my habits had Miranda and our friends crawling all over me. I was thankful they did care after all, but since the accident, I was tired of hearing, "Are you feeling okay?" or "Don't you need to talk about it?" Truth was, I didn't feel okay, and I certainly didn't want to talk about it.

I was tired of being under a microscope. From the minute I

woke up in the hospital, everyone wanted to know what it was like to be dead. I had no clue. I never saw the tunnel of light or heard the voices of loved ones beyond the grave calling my name. The only recollection I had was waking up surrounded by my bug-eyed friends and feeling like I had been in a very deep sleep. And even though I didn't have one of those experiences, I was left with the feeling—knowing that this life was just a precursor to another very real existence.

"I'm gonna pass out or puke," I heard a woman say over the whir of the treadmill. The mirror I was facing gave me a full view of the gym. I could see a woman in a lunge position. She looked up at Jade red-faced and said, "I appear to be stuck." Jade gave her a hand, and she slowly stood upright. "I think I blew out an ass cheek," she whispered loudly. I chewed the inside of my cheek, staving off a laugh as I watched the owner of the blown ass cheek limp toward the locker room.

I looked back at my own figure in the mirror and was sad to note that I wasn't the woman I was in my twenties and early thirties. Years of late nights filled with meals and drinks were catching up, but that had come to a screeching halt. I started to jog for two reasons—the first being that I wanted to get rid of the soft fold of skin that hung just over the waistband of my pants. The second, and probably most important, I wasn't in a hurry to return to an empty house and try to figure out something to do until I went to bed.

"You know, if you vary your workout, you might see more results," someone said a while later. I noticed that Perfection Personified was standing next to the treadmill as I did my cool-down walk. "I've seen you here at least three nights a week, and you always do the same workout."

"I'm a creature of habit, I guess." I switched off the machine and hopped off.

"I'm Corrine Verner, but everyone just calls me Jade." She thrust out her hand, and I stared at it awkwardly.

"I'm a…germaphobe, please don't take it personally."

She gave me one of those half grins that I'd seen her giving everyone else in the gym and a nod. "I understand."

"I used to jog around the neighborhood where I live or on the beach. But my best friend was given a membership by her partner when she started to gain weight around her midsection. She's the redhead. You might've seen her."

Jade nodded.

"I've been tagging along, and I guess I haven't really been truly invested in my workouts." I shrugged as Jade looked at me as though she doubted I did more than sit on the couch.

She folded her arms. "Since you're paying a monthly fee, don't you think you should get what you're paying for?"

Her stance and the way she spoke put me on the defensive. I felt like she was saying, "Get with the program or get out."

I crossed my arms, too. "Are you about to put a sales pitch on me? Maybe offer your services as a trainer?"

"Not at all. I was going to offer to write up an exercise plan for you depending on what your goals are." She shrugged. "That's all I can offer. My client list is booked."

I was sure it was loaded with people who wanted to look like her or be with her. "How much is that going to cost me?"

Jade's green eyes narrowed. "Nothing, it comes with the membership. No one explained that to you when you joined?"

I wanted to ask if anyone ever explained that she was supposed to be nice to the customer. Attitude was coming off of her in waves, and I felt myself wanting to match it. "They probably did, but like I said, I haven't been invested in the workout. I'm just a tagalong to keep Miranda company."

She cocked her head to the side, uncrossed her arms, and put her hands behind her back. "Well, I hope you'll consider my offer and tell your friend Miranda I'll be happy to write a plan for her, too."

"I'll consider it." I tossed my towel over my shoulder. "Nice to meet you." I turned and walked away.

"I'm here till nine each weeknight," Jade called after me.

"I know," I said over my shoulder and kept walking.

The next morning, I opened my shop, which consisted of filling the cash drawer of the register and propping a chair in front of the door. March in Florida could be a mixed bag. We'd go a week or two with spring-like temps, trees and shrubs would bud, then there'd be a frost. On this day, spring was in the air, and I let it fill my shop with its warmth and pollen.

Snowbirds kept me afloat during the off-season as they enjoyed the cold months in their beach houses. The summer brought with it a whole new clientele—those who rented the beach houses the snowbirds had vacated. This and That was exactly that. My store was a cornucopia of beach décor, not the kitschy stuff sold in shell shops like ashtrays covered in seashells or T-shirts. There was really no call for that in Panacea, though the convenience stores sold a modest amount. I sold prints and wicker furniture, crab traps that had seen their last day in the sea, things you could look at and be reminded of a world that survived off the Gulf waters.

Crawfordville, Medart, Panacea, and Ochlockonee Bay were small towns meshed together on Highway 98, and if you weren't familiar with the area, you wouldn't know that you'd passed into one from the other. For me, it was the best of both worlds—small-town country living with a beach hidden well behind the oaks and pines. And if I wanted something more, I could drive the thirty minutes into Tallahassee.

"You're letting a lot of dust and pollen into your shop."

I looked up from the counter where I was weaving one of the prettier shells that I'd found on the beach into a necklace and smiled at Miranda as she walked in. "No lives to save this morning?"

"Actually, I'm fresh off an abdominal pain call, my first of the morning." Miranda grimaced. "She threw up on my shoes. It's not ten o'clock, and I'm already in my spare uniform."

I wrinkled my nose and kept my distance.

"I showered, too, you weenie."

I looked around for her. "Where's your partner?"

Miranda grinned. "He's sleeping off a hangover in the unit. Got into a fight with his girlfriend again and drowned his anger in a bottle of vodka. Needless to say, our patient's stomach issues took a toll on him. In all my years as a paramedic, I don't think

I've ever seen that shade of green on a human." She leaned on the counter and toyed with one of the necklaces I'd already finished. "So how'd it go with Jade last night?"

I kept my focus on my project. "She offered to write up a workout plan for us. According to her, we're not going to see results if we keep doing the same thing every time we go to the gym."

"So you made a move."

"Yep, and she's as arrogant as you assumed." I looked up at Miranda and grinned. "You won't be able to live vicariously through me with that one."

"Shit. Marty is going to be so disappointed. I told her you were working your magic. You're slipping, little player. There was a time your charm was irresistible. But that one, well, she's a tough ticket even for you."

I laughed. "Yes, the kid was shot down, but she lives to ride another day."

"You're a complete womanizer. Don't you ever get tired of that?"

I shook my head and continued weaving. "If I settled down, I wouldn't be able to entertain you with my exploits."

Miranda tugged on the loose end of the necklace I was working on. "I'm serious. Don't you ever think about having someone to share your life, your secrets with?"

I sighed and sat back on my stool behind the counter. "This is one of those conversations, isn't it?" Everyone in our group of friends was a part of a couple. I was the exception. "Sometimes I wonder if y'all want me to settle down and be happy or if I pose a threat to your coupledom. You all see me going out and worry that maybe you or your partners might be tempted to want to enjoy the lifestyle I do."

"That was bitchy."

"You're right, I apologize."

"You're thirty-eight, it's a reasonable question." Miranda didn't look at me. Instead she scratched at a piece of clear tape stuck to the glass top of the counter with her thumbnail. "Why are you afraid to commit? What is it?"

"I have no idea," I answered truthfully. "I don't dwell on it."

"Self-preservation. It keeps us from doing or thinking about a lot of things, doesn't it?"

I tilted my head as I regarded Miranda. "You sound like a shrink."

She tapped the counter with her thumb and pushed back, looking at me. "Because I've been seeing a therapist. I started after we got back from vacation. After you…" She looked away with discomfort showing plainly on her face.

The revelation stunned me. "Why?"

Miranda folded her arms and stared at something on the wall. "I froze up out there. I…couldn't do CPR on you…I forgot how." She took a deep shuddering breath. "When we got you out of the water and I saw your face, my mind went blank."

I felt detached like Miranda was talking about one of her patients. My only recollection was waking up in the hospital. "Well, you were in shock. That makes sense, right?"

Tears filled Miranda's eyes as she finally looked at me. "You're my best friend, a sister, really, and I couldn't save you. Some stranger fresh out of Advanced First-Aid had to start what I couldn't. All the years of training and experience trickled out of my ears, and I was useless."

"Hey, look—"

"And you won't talk about any of it," Miranda said angrily as she wiped her eyes on her sleeve. "We talk about everything. I've lost that connection with you."

"I don't remember anything. I don't—"

"But surely, it changed you, impacted you in some way." Miranda clenched her fists and stopped short of pounding them on the counter. "You were dead, no pulse. A person doesn't come back from something like that without being affected in some way."

All the air in my lungs felt like it evaporated. I couldn't speak. For the first time since we'd returned from West Virginia, I couldn't ignore the pain on Miranda's face. I couldn't form the lie that I'd told countless times since the accident. I sat mute while Miranda stared at me, waiting.

"Good morning," a woman said as she poked her head in the door. "Everything okay in here?"

"Ah, yes." I smiled weakly. "The driver of the ambulance out front is a friend of mine and just visiting." I pointed at Miranda, who did her best to smile. "Come on in and look around. If you have any questions, just let me know." I looked back at Miranda when the customer disappeared among the rows of shelves. "We'll talk about this later, I promise."

Miranda made another attempt at a smile. "I'll come by tomorrow after my shift. I'll bring breakfast."

I couldn't sleep that night. When I closed my eyes, I could see the misery on Miranda's face, and the guilt that followed consumed me. I knew she was struggling. I sensed it whenever we were together. She'd tried many times to talk about that day, but I'd always changed the subject, never considering that she needed to purge her soul.

We weren't the affectionate type of friends who hugged often or draped an arm around a shoulder unless one of us was really hurting. Marty told me that before I had awakened in the hospital that Miranda had nearly crawled up in the bed and held me as she cried her eyes out. The only affection I'd seen from her since was a fist bump after I came to and got my wits back. For that, I was grateful.

Had the contact been any longer than that fleeting touch of fists, I would've seen and felt what she had witnessed that day. I'd caught glimpses from the others when they hugged me or touched me. Through their eyes, for the briefest moments, I saw my lifeless body lying on the ice staring back at me.

Chapter 2

I didn't open the shop at the usual time. Instead I put the plastic clock on the door indicating that I would open at noon. Miranda would see this and know to come around back to the house. I knew the conversation we were due to have would be emotional, and for me, showing emotion was a rarity. I had learned at a very young age to hide my feelings. As a grown woman, I was a master. I'd spent most of my life behind a mask of stoicism. There was only one person who had seen beyond it, and I watched as she walked up on my porch and let herself in as she always did.

"I have doughnuts and chocolate milk. We'll work it off tonight, no worries." Miranda walked past me where I was sitting on the couch with a cup of coffee and went into the kitchen. She returned a moment later with two glasses and a roll of paper towels.

"How was your shift?" I asked as I watched her pour the milk.

"Mercifully quiet." Miranda wiped her hands on her pants. "We had a total of three calls and all before ten last night. I'm rested and ready to go to the gym tonight and work off the fluff this breakfast is sure to cause." She dipped her hand into her shirt pocket and pulled out a handful of pictures. "I meant to give these to you yesterday."

I took the prints and thumbed through them until I came to one of Miranda and me sitting side by side at a table. Miranda's hair bright red and spiky stood out in contrast to my shoulder-length brown, her eyes bright and blue and mine dark. Her skin tone pale and mine olive. It was apparent we weren't blood related, but we were sisters nevertheless.

"I'm gonna frame this one." I took it out of the group and laid it on the coffee table.

She smiled. "I framed mine, too."

I set my coffee aside and picked up my glass of milk. As I downed half of it, I was reminded of when we were kids. We shared a chocolate milk the first day we met. We were twelve, and my aunt had just moved us into the neighborhood. Aunt Judith was not particularly pleased with her new digs. Her two-bedroom condo wasn't large enough for her and two kids she never expected to have. The house was bigger and afforded us another bedroom, but it wasn't in an area she would've chosen if she had a choice. "I always thought I'd move up, not down," she would complain.

She and my mom weren't close, but after my mother's death, she was the only option. Our father had long since gone, and no one knew where to find him. Judith was not comfortable with the role of mother and often spent her evenings in her bedroom with the door closed after dinner. Five years my senior, Colin, my brother, didn't have to stay long. On his eighteenth birthday, he went into the military, leaving me alone with an aunt who was biding her time until she could kick me out of the nest and get on with her life.

Cecilia Donahue, Miranda's mother, adopted me as her own, though not legally. I spent more time in the Donahue home than I did with Judith, especially after Colin left. Momma Donahue, as I called her then, simply became Mom over the years. She and Miranda were there for me through every achievement and disappointment, and had it not been for their love and acceptance, I was fairly certain I would've never made it to adulthood.

"Talk to me," Miranda said without preamble.

I felt my mouth go dry. It took me a while to say, "It has affected me."

"Bad dreams, or do you contemplate your mortality more?"

"Neither." I tried to muster a smile, but the muscles in my face wouldn't comply. I had always trusted Miranda with my innermost secrets, but this…made me question my own sanity.

Miranda would respect my wish to keep it between us, I knew that. She'd give advice without judgment, but...

"Just tell me."

I looked into her clear blue eyes and chewed my bottom lip. "The effect the incident had on me," I began, sounding clinical to my own ears, "left me with an odd byproduct."

Doughnuts and chocolate milk momentarily forgotten, Miranda sat literally on the edge of her seat waiting.

"I've done some research. It's not really all that uncommon for people who have had near-death experiences. People come back with all sorts of oddities, then some have nothing at all. I think—"

"Quit with the foreplay and let me have it," Miranda said impatiently.

I held up my hand and looked at it. "If I touch you, I can see...things."

Miranda's pale brows rose. "What things?"

"After we came home from West Virginia...I met a woman online." Miranda rolled her eyes at this. I met most of the women I dated on the Net. "We met at a restaurant in Tallahassee, and everything was going great until I touched her hand while talking. And then I was in her car, felt the wheel beneath my hands and her frustration with the traffic that was making her run late." I laughed. It sounded so strange in the retelling. I had trouble believing it myself. "It was like I was in her body as she walked into her house and changed for our date. Jeans or skirt, blue or gray? And then I heard a voice, and it felt familiar. Her husband was in the kitchen, and when she kissed him, I felt the brush of stubble against my lips. The lie was so easily delivered, 'I'm going out with the girls, remember? Don't wait up.'" I looked at Miranda, who sat quietly, stunned. "I'll never forget what her face looked like when I stood, tossed a few bills on the table, and walked out of the restaurant without another word."

Miranda cleared her throat. "Was this an isolated incident or have there been others?"

I nodded. "Deb, she hugged me when I got out of the hospital. I felt the ice against her stomach, felt the coldness of her hands while she held on to your boots. The shock, the confusion. It was so strong I had to pull away from her. I think maybe she thought I blamed her."

Miranda exhaled loudly and leaned back in her chair. "This has been going on for two months, and you haven't said a word."

"I thought I was going crazy. I needed time to cope with it on my own before I could tell you about it."

"I knew you were keeping something from me. I felt like there was a wall between us." Miranda nodded as though everything was beginning to make sense. "The others have noticed it, too. You've never been really affectionate, but lately, you've shied away from the group. Marty says she noticed how you deftly avoid being hugged. We all figured that maybe you were riding the razor's edge of emotion, and affection would cause it to spill over."

"Y'all have spent a lot of time talking about me."

"Because we care," Miranda said pointedly. "Don't mistake that for going behind your back. We've just been trying to figure you out. You would do the same, you know it."

I nodded. "I don't want them to know, not even Marty."

Miranda stared at me, her eyes narrowed from time to time. A few minutes passed before she spoke. "Do you think that's fair? They don't know what you say you can do. If you touch them, you'll be invading their privacy. Your closest friends should at least have the option of whether they want their secrets exposed to you or not."

It was my turn to stare. I dissected every sentence carefully in my mind, reading into what she said and the underlying meaning. "You don't believe me. You think I'm using this as an excuse to avoid everyone while I deal with the supposed 'razor's edge of emotion.'"

Miranda shot me that narrow-eyed look she used when her defenses were up, then she smiled. "When you don't want to have to deal with something, you shut it off. You pack it in a box and store it in the deep recesses of your mind." She cocked her head to the side. "I've never known you to deliberately lie to me, though."

"I'm not lying."

Miranda stood and joined me on the couch. She thrust out her hand. "Touch me."

I stared down at her it, studied the fine lines on her palm, buying time, because I knew what I'd see. More than wanting to prove myself to her, I felt I owed her. She'd been traumatized enough about that day that she'd sought out professional help. My best friend, my sister needed me to understand her as much as I needed her to understand me, so I took her hand.

Gut-wrenching horror seized my chest. Lonna was struggling. I could hear her grunting as she wrestled with a green piece of cloth. Numb from the cold, my bare hands barely felt the boots I was clinging to white-knuckled. I was shivering, not from the cold and wetness that penetrated my clothes, but at the prospect of loss so profound it made me physically ill.

Lonna wasn't making headway. She didn't have the upper body strength it would take to pull the water-logged body from the water. I prayed the ice would hold as I tugged my boot free of Deb's grasp and began to crawl. When I reached the opening in the ice, I saw the dark hair plastered down on a blue face. The eyes wide open, mouth gaping. I felt my hands plunging into the icy water grasping for anything I could cling to. The lifeless body felt like ice itself and just as heavy as we pulled, pure adrenaline giving us strength we didn't possess.

Through Miranda's eyes, I looked down at myself, hardly recognizable. My mind blank. I released her hand with a gasp and quickly began retelling everything as I saw and felt it as though I were recounting a dream I was afraid I'd forget. Miranda blinked at the barrage of information. I saw the realization dawn on her face, her eyes widen. Her bottom lip began to tremble as I described in detail her feelings, her fear.

After I finished, we sat quietly as tears streamed down her cheeks. I wanted to cry. For the first time in my life, I wanted to release the emotion pounding inside my chest, but I couldn't. Instead, I stared at the floor as the memory of what I'd seen flashed through my mind.

"Oh, my God." Miranda sank back onto the couch and covered her face with her hands.

I let her cry, afraid to touch her. Afraid of what else I might see. "I want to…comfort you, but…"

"I know," Miranda said through her tears.

I smiled ruefully. "I've been thinking about what this will mean for me from now on. Can you imagine what sex would be like? Full body contact, and I'm watching videos of that person's life. I'll never have an orgasm I didn't personally cause again."

"Oh," Miranda said with a sniff. "That's a real concentration breaker, isn't it?"

"Yeah." My shoulders sagged. "I'm either going to have to become a hermit or live my life telling one lie after the other to hide what I've become."

"Maybe you could wear gloves," Miranda said, sounding more like herself.

"Welder's gloves maybe, something thick like that." I was actually considering it.

"Maybe you can learn to control it. You've always been really good at blocking things out. That might just work to your advantage."

"I understand why you needed to see a shrink." I glanced at her quickly and looked away. "If that had been you, I would've been pretty messed up."

Miranda sighed long and loud. "Nothing has ever scared me that bad." She reached out to touch me, then let her hand drop in her lap. "Are you telling me everything? You didn't have an out-of-body experience while you were…down."

"I did see some angels. They were wearing Krispy Kreme hats, and as they flapped their wings, hot doughnuts appeared." I banged one of the doughnuts Miranda brought. "Unlike these, they weren't made of stone."

Miranda threw back her head and laughed. "You are such an asshole. I love ya."

The gym was full, and Miranda and I waited to use leg presses. We stood side by side careful not to brush against each other. "Wouldn't you like to touch P.P. and see what all her secrets are? Probably one sexual escapade after another." Miranda chuckled.

"It'd be like interactive porn." She lowered her voice. "You'd definitely have an orgasm that way."

P.P. was the nickname we'd given Jade—Perfection Personified. She was across the room working with one of her clients wearing nothing but a pair of black spandex shorts and matching sports bra. I watched the muscles bunch and move under perfectly tanned skin, one part lust, the other envy. My arms had toned nicely, but the muscles there did not compare to what Jade was working with. Her stomach had that washboard look you only saw in commercials advertising diet aids or workout equipment.

"Thanks for putting up with my jokes," Miranda said seriously. "We've spent the day grappling with the magnitude of this…thing, and I just needed a release. You know I'm not making light of what you're dealing with."

"Oh, that goes without saying. I've been dealing with this for two months, so it's refreshing to sort of make fun of it."

Miranda didn't speak again until we had completed our first rep on the leg press. I lay stomach down on the one next to her and watched Jade demonstrate how to use the elliptical machine to a man who already looked weary.

"So what do you think? Should we take her up on her offer and let her write a plan for us?" Miranda asked between grunts.

"Couldn't hurt, I guess. Might as well get what we're paying for. But you're gonna have to ask her for the both of us. My pride will not allow me to acquiesce."

We finished our workout and loitered until Jade wrapped up with her client. Miranda wasted no time in her approach. I stood back and watched them talk until Miranda motioned for me to follow. Jade led us back to a tiny cramped office barely large enough to accommodate the desk and a chair that sat in front of it. I stood in the corner while Miranda took the seat.

"I have a questionnaire for you to fill out." Jade fished around in her desk and produced two blue pieces of paper. "Sloan, you're welcome to take my chair, and I'll go find another one while you work on the questions."

She left us alone without another word, and I took the seat careful not to lean back and leave my sweat all over her chair.

I checked the boxes next to the areas of my body I wanted to work on, then another indicating how much time I was willing to invest. Miranda and I hesitated as we read over the ones concerning diet.

"Should we disclose how much junk food we really eat?" She might suggest a diet." Miranda paled at the thought.

"Are we coming here to pacify Marty, or do we really want to get into shape?"

Miranda thought for a moment. "I really would love to lose this paunch in my stomach." She grimaced. "That means diet."

"We can still have pizza and doughnuts," I said, trying to reassure us both. "Just not as often. We've never really been good at practicing moderation."

Miranda agreed.

"Let's listen to what she has to say."

"So you're saying be honest." Miranda grimaced again and resumed her focus on the questionnaire.

Jade returned to her office about five minutes after we finished our paperwork. She set the extra chair next to Miranda and sat down. I watched as she picked up Miranda's questionnaire and read it over, her expression impassive. Next, she scooped up mine and scrutinized it before laying it in her lap with Miranda's.

"Let's talk about diet first," she said, looking at us. I heard Miranda whimper.

"Portion control, and of course, what you're eating needs to change if you want to achieve the things you've listed." She looked at Miranda with what I construed was compassion. "I think it's fairly obvious you have a sweet tooth."

"I have a mouth full of them," Miranda confessed with a blush.

"I imagine being a paramedic is difficult when it comes to diet. You run calls in the middle of the night, then you're hungry, so you grab a snack from whatever is open." Jade tilted her head to the side. "Probably raid the vending machines in the hospital for sugary snacks, then go back to the station and sleep."

"Bingo," Miranda said with a nod.

"Would you consider packing healthy snacks to take to work with you? Something to munch on during those times?"

"We have no idea what a healthy snack is," I said, drawing Jade's attention. I shrugged. "Okay, fruit, but that's not really filling."

"I agree, but fruit is a good substitute for a candy bar. I have a list of snacks that will satisfy hunger, too, and don't contain as much sugar." She looked at Miranda again. "Will you try that?"

"Yes," Miranda said with a nod.

Jade looked back at me then. "You appear to have a habit of not eating during the day." She glanced down at my paper. "You're probably busy with work, then at the end of the day, you're starving and eat whatever you find in the fridge or order pizza. Often you eat way too much to make up for what you didn't get during the day."

"Bingo." Miranda pointed at me. "She nailed your ass."

"I can write up a meal plan," Jade continued. "You'll have to shop, both of you will, but if you get into the habit of eating healthier, you'll see the results you want." She looked down at the papers in her lap again. "I'll also write up an exercise plan that will target the areas you want to work. If you're unfamiliar with any of the machines, I or any of the trainers will be happy to demonstrate for you."

Miranda and I nodded our agreement.

"Set some goals for yourselves. I can help with that or you can do it on your own, but I think it's easier if you have something to work toward." She looked at Miranda then. "As I've told Sloan, my client list is full, but I can do some rearranging if you need extra help. I can also suggest other trainers who have openings if you want to go that route."

"We'll work from the plan you come up with," I said before Miranda could speak. "If we don't see results, we might consider enlisting the help of a trainer." I looked at Miranda, and she gave me a thumbs-up.

"Great." Jade stood, and Miranda and I followed suit. She shook Miranda's hand but withdrew when she turned to me. "I remember, germaphobe." She tucked her hand behind her back and shot me her half smile.

I nodded. "Thanks for taking the time, Jade."

Miranda and I walked down the hall together, holding all comment until we were outside. The ride home wasn't that long, but I'd had to pee before the meeting with Jade, and I decided I couldn't wait. "Gotta visit the potty," I said to Miranda. I turned on one heel and slammed into Jade. We fell against the wall, and her arms went around my waist to steady me. The contact was surprising and brief, but it didn't stop the flashes that entered my mind or the wash of feeling that encompassed me.

I stepped back on shaky legs. "I'm sorry. I didn't know you were behind me."

"That's okay." Jade pushed off the wall. "Are you all right?" she asked as she looked me over.

"I'm fine, sorry again." I half ran to the bathroom. In the privacy of the stall, I hovered over the toilet seat. In that case, I really was a germaphobe. Through Jade's eyes, I saw the road before me. I didn't recognize it, and I was fairly certain she didn't, either. Though brief, the image really didn't reveal anything, but the feelings that came with it made me uncomfortable. She didn't want to be there. Fear and revulsion coalesced into painful resignation. None of it made sense to me, but I did know one thing—Jade was unhappy.

"So what did you see when you bumped into her?" Miranda asked when I joined her in the parking lot.

"Just a quick glimpse of her riding in someone's car. She didn't seem happy about it."

"Probably one of those dates you have—a lot. She was with someone she didn't like and was trying to get out of it."

"Probably," I said with a nod.

Normally, our way of saying good night was a fist bump. In the habit, Miranda raised her fist, then awkwardly tucked her hand behind her back. "I'm trying to get used to this. My mind has been going ninety miles an hour since you told me." She stuffed her hands in the pockets of her gym pants. "It won't always be so awkward. We'll work through this...like we've always worked through things."

I wanted to hug her. Perhaps another byproduct of my experience, I craved to give and receive affection, and now ironically, I couldn't. "Thanks." I opened the door to my car and smiled back at her. "Give Marty a kiss for me, will ya?"

Miranda looked at me oddly for a second before saying, "Will do."

Chapter 3

A few days later, Jade produced a diet and workout plan for Miranda and me. Dutifully, I went to the grocery store that night after the gym and purchased the foods on the list. I was pleasantly surprised to note it didn't include wing of bat or eye of newt as I had anticipated. Most were meats and veggies I already liked but was too lazy to take the time to cook. That had to change. I'd known it for a while.

It was late when I got home, so I had turkey on wheat with slices of dill pickle instead of condiments. I washed it down with a glass of water, showered, and went to bed. I thought I had a pretty decent handle on loneliness. Surrounded by friends who had companions, I recognized the empty feeling often. I'd keep it at bay by going home and getting online. Usually, by the next weekend, I'd have a date, someone to occupy my time and sometimes my bed. But in the quiet hours when I lay staring at the ceiling as I did that night, I felt it creeping in, as familiar to me as the pillow beneath my head. But unlike the pillow, it brought me no comfort.

Marty and Miranda had been together for six years. Deb and Angel for three, Lonna and Paige had just celebrated their first anniversary. Miranda, Deb, and Lonna were my friends, and I'd watched each of them fall in love and enter the world of coupledom. I'd seen lovers come and go, but now it all seemed different. They were settled, happy, content.

I never bothered to question why I hadn't done the same. I told myself and them that it just wasn't my thing. Miranda knew better, and I did, too, even though I denied it to everyone, including myself. I was scared. My mother, brother, and ultimately, my aunt had left me. Even Momma Donahue when she succumbed to complications from diabetes. I was afraid to invest my feelings in someone, even though I'd done it with Miranda. I had no choice, really. She wove her way into my heart over time. But to trust to hope…that was just too scary for me, the price way too high to pay.

I ate breakfast according to Jade's meal plan, then I went to the store and opened up. I felt good, energized, ready to face the day with the loneliness of night far behind me. I'd no sooner sat down to craft another necklace when a couple of women walked into my shop. They were middle-aged and wealthy looking, perhaps a couple of snowbirds looking for a few things to spruce up the winter nest before flying to their summer homes in cooler climates. I greeted them with a smile and gave my usual spiel, "Look around and let me know if you need anything."

One came to the counter where I was working. "How much are the Adirondack chairs out front?"

"They're seventy-five, unless you're looking at the ones that are painted, and they're a hundred. Buy two of either and get twenty percent off."

The woman with way too many dangly bracelets looked back at her friend, who nodded. "We'll definitely take two of the painted ones, but I'll have to come back this afternoon when my husband comes in from fishing. He has the truck, you see."

I nodded and smiled.

"You'll load them, won't you? He has a bad back."

"Yes, ma'am, of course."

Her gaze moved to the rack of necklaces I had painstakingly hand-woven the best shells I could find into. The corner of her mouth sagged. "Chintzy."

And I said in my mind only, *Asshole*.

She strolled off looking at other things, then called to me from somewhere in the back of the store. When I found them, she and her friend were admiring an antique surfboard mounted on the wall too high for them to reach. "That would look perfect on the wall of my sun porch. Could you get it down for us? I'd like to have a closer look."

"Certainly." I grabbed my footstool, took the board down, and held it for their inspection.

"Is this real or is it just made to look that way?"

"It's real—" The air went out of my lungs in a rush when the woman laid her hand on my arm to ask another question.

I was in an office, and a man in a white lab coat was sitting next to me. He gently took my hand in his. "I know the chemo and radiation were hard to endure the last time—"

I felt her sadness, worry for her husband and children. She spoke, and I could feel the words passing over my tongue as if I'd said them myself. "Not this time. I'm going to live out my last days doing things I enjoy, not lying in bed or hovering over a toilet. When the pain becomes too unmanageable, you'll help me with that, won't you?"

The connection broke when she released me. "Miss, are you okay?"

I stared at her speechless for so long that the women exchanged nervous glances. "I'm sorry," I said with a shake of my head. "Got a lot on my mind, lost my train of thought." My hands trembled as I looked down at the board. Had she told me she was dying, I'd have felt sympathy, but to see it, experience it tore a hole in my heart. "I'd like you to have this…if you want it. Free of charge."

The women exchanged glances again.

"I got it cheap." That was a lie. "And since you're buying the chairs, I'd like to throw it in. It's perfect for a sun porch."

"Well, thank you," the woman said, still looking stunned.

"I'll put it behind the counter, and when you come back for the chairs, I'll load it for you." I walked away before I started crying.

"You finally sold the board." Miranda walked into the store and looked at the bare spot on the wall. "Bet you lost money on it."

I stared down at the counter. "I did."

"How much? Was it bad? Does your ass burn?"

I laughed at her choice of words. "I gave it away."

"What?" Miranda's jaw sagged. "I've been hounding you for years to let me buy that board for what you paid for it."

"I know." I looked at her sadly. "She touched me."

Miranda was winding up for a tirade. Her face fell. "What did you see?"

"She's terminally ill with cancer, I think." I shivered as that memory flashed through my mind again.

Miranda swallowed and smacked her lips. "I see. Maybe... you really should consider the welding gloves and perhaps a suit of armor."

I scrubbed at my face. "Maybe I should hire someone to work in the store full time and I'll stay home."

Miranda looked at me and said sarcastically, "You can't afford to, especially now that you're giving all your shit away."

"What am I going to do?" I asked miserably. "I can't always avoid human contact unless I hide away."

"Not an option you should consider. I mean, I won't let you consider it." Miranda reached out to touch my hand and hesitated. I watched as it dawned on her just how dismal my situation was becoming. "We have to figure this out."

"How're we gonna do that?" I hoped she'd done better at figuring it out than I had in the last two months.

"Practice on me. Let's get together after you close the store and see what we can do."

Miranda spent one of two days off milling around the store with me, and she took care of the few customers who came in. After, we loaded the Adirondack chairs for the customer I'd given my surfboard to. Miranda hugged the bewildered woman twice and her husband once. We went back to the house, and I whipped up dinner according to Jade's meal plan. I didn't have to ask if Marty minded coming home to an empty house. She'd grown used to having to share Miranda with me.

I wasn't as enthusiastic as Miranda was, but by the end of dinner, I did have an inkling of hope. Maybe I could control it, at least enough to tolerate brief contact and maybe even a hug. I watched as Miranda took our plates to the sink and stuffed a cucumber slice into her mouth. When she returned to the table, she was all business.

"I think you should touch me for a minute and get used to it. Then clear your head and touch me again but briefly until you can get a grip on your mind."

"Okay." I watched as she put her hand on the table in front of me. I glanced at her face, and she gave me that "go ahead" look. It didn't matter if I touched her with my fingertips or entire hand, the second my flesh contacted with hers, the movie began.

Through Miranda, I was standing at the graveside of Momma Donahue alone. The crowd that had gathered there had all slipped away, leaving me to stare at the last thing I would remember of my mother. A sob escaped my chest as the summer breeze caressed my skin, and the smell of flowers filled my senses.

I knew she was sick. I knew she was dying, and as prepared as I thought I was when that day came, it took me completely by surprise. Nothing prepared you for the loss of a parent, especially when you'd only had one your whole life. I looked back over my shoulder…and there I stood. Seeing myself through Miranda's eyes was a shock. I looked so small standing there in my black suit, my hands going into pockets only to reappear seconds later. But on my face was the same pain that was tearing Miranda up inside, and she knew it. Miranda walked over to where I stood and took me in her arms. I felt what it was like to hold me, such an odd sensation. Probably the most stunning thing I gleaned from the vision was Miranda's feelings. During that hug, she accepted as I did on that day that we only had each other.

"I don't know if I can do this." I sat back in my chair feeling like I did the day of the funeral.

"What did you see?"

"You at Mom's funeral. Remember when we were alone at the graveside and we hugged?"

Miranda nodded and averted her eyes. Her mother had been gone for nearly eight years, but she still couldn't talk about her without getting misty. "So you saw me in the cemetery."

"No, not just saw you. I was you. I felt everything you felt in those moments. I think that's the real downside to this. I'm in your body. I feel and see it all as if we were the same person." I scratched my arm for an itch that wasn't there, needing something to do.

"I was thinking about that time we collected all those glass drink bottles and turned them in for the deposit so we could buy cigarettes." Miranda grinned. "As I recall, you puked after the first puff."

I smiled at the memory, but my mind was on my problem. "You know what's weird? When I first touched you, I felt your excitement over what we would come up with, then it all switched like it does in a dream. I feel your emotions now and the ones you had in the cemetery then."

Miranda looked at me for a second, clearly not listening to a word. "Touch me again, but this time, focus on the memory of us smoking. I'll think of it, too."

I did as she asked, and soon I felt the burning in my chest and the roiling of my stomach as I in Miranda's body inhaled the smoke. It tasted nasty in my mouth, but I was determined to look cool. Watching through Miranda's eyes, I saw myself inhale from my own cigarette, my face contorted, but I made another attempt. Then I was retching. I felt Miranda's amusement, felt the laugh rumble from my chest and my stomach whirling.

"You were sick, too, you ass. Why didn't you tell me it nauseated you?"

Miranda looked at me in surprise as I smacked my lips with the taste of the cigarette still on my tongue.

"See, you can control it. You picked a memory, then you were there." Miranda slammed her hands on the table. "First experiment successful. Now, part two. Touch me again, and whatever comes to your mind, reject it. Do it quickly at first."

I touched her hand again and looked down at myself lying in a hospital bed. I knew I was okay, but I needed...I needed to be close and hand holding wasn't enough. I felt my knees press into the mattress...

"You're not stopping." Miranda pulled her hand away.

"I can't help it. It's just so weird when I'm looking at myself."

Miranda put her hand back down. "Try harder."

I lay mine atop hers, and I immediately saw myself in that hospital bed again. I clamped my eyes shut, trying to push the image away, and it worked when I pictured my favorite spot on the beach. What did not fade were the feelings. The internal pleading, *Please don't leave me. Please don't ever leave me.*

I shoved away from the table angrily. "This isn't going to work. I'm so screwed!"

Miranda watched as I paced back and forth, then spoke softly. "It's not going to work the first time. It's going to take practice."

"I don't want to practice." I paced some more and finally calmed. "Not tonight. No more tonight, please."

"I should be getting home anyway." Miranda stood and stretched, then she held out her fist. I looked at it a moment before I banged it with mine. For a fleeting second, I felt her disappointment in me.

Chapter 4

"I hate lunges." Miranda grunted alongside me. "All this equipment and we're squatting around like chickens trying to lay an egg. And all the protein she has us eating makes me want to fart twenty-four seven."

"How nice for Marty."

"If I blow one, I'm blaming it on you." Miranda grunted again, and I feared she would deliver on her promise.

"Looking good, ladies," Jade said as she passed by. "Keep your backs straight."

"Piss off, P.P.," Miranda said under her breath.

"I wonder if she does lunges and how many she had to do to get that tone in her thighs." I watched the muscles flex as she moved more with envy, less lust.

"She probably does all sorts of shit." Miranda stood up straight with a groan when we reached the wall. "Obviously, she's a masochist and gets off on the pain. Or maybe she's a sadist and likes hurting us."

"Shut up," I said as I saw Jade head our way.

"I think y'all might be sweating more than usual," she said with that crooked smile that only showed a couple of teeth and never reached her eyes.

"Then I guess we're doing it right." I looked at Miranda, who grunted. "You have to at least give us an A for effort."

"Absolutely." Jade put her hands on her hips. "I suggest soaking in a tub with some Epsom salt for the soreness."

"Getting out of the tub is going to be the problem." Miranda rubbed her lower back, then her neck. She jerked a thumb in my direction. "Unlike me, she doesn't have anyone to pull her out, and I'm in no shape to rush over and do it."

Jade shot us that grin again. "Well, there's always the fire department," she said as she sauntered off.

Miranda stared after her. "Ya know, I thought she was really nice when she offered to do our plans, but the more I get to know her, I think that bitch has it in for us."

I was inclined to agree. After talking to a person, I kind of got a bead on their personality, sort of had them figured out, but Jade was an enigma. One minute, she was brash, bordering on flat-out rude, then the next, friendly, almost caring, then right back to butthole.

I caught her watching us a few times when we were going through the program. She would give a slight nod when our eyes met. And then I found myself contemplating something that astonished me. I had actually begun to think of ways to touch her. Maybe a casual bump, but that wouldn't be enough to see what was in that head of hers. I realized what I was thinking was the equivalent of putting my ear against her office door or listening in on a private phone call. I chastised myself accordingly and focused on my self-imposed torture.

But the opportunity presented itself anyway, and shamefully, I took it. As if in slow motion, I watched a man turn with one of those steel hand weights. Jade was focused on a client, and they collided. The weight dropped onto her foot. One of the other trainers was there immediately, gingerly pulling off her shoe as Jade rocked back and forth, puffing out her pain. I walked behind her and laid a hand on her shoulder.

The pain on the top right side of my foot was so intense that my knee buckled, and I ended up squatting behind her. As the images took shape, the pain receded, and I took from her things she would've never offered a stranger like me. The connection broke between us when two of her fellow trainers hefted her up and carried her away. I sat there feeling ashamed of what I'd done and crushed by what I'd seen.

Miranda appeared in front of me as I got to my feet. "I saw you," she whispered. "What are you doing?"

I wiped at the sweat on my face with both hands to cover my shame. I couldn't look at Miranda. I turned and walked out of the gym.

She caught me before I was able to get into my car and put her hand on the door. "I asked you what you were doing," she said calmly.

"I don't know." I turned and looked past her shoulder, still unable to meet her gaze. "I was curious. Her behavior is kind of off, right?"

Miranda nodded. "Yeah, she's odd."

"The whole time we were working out, I kept thinking about her, and the more I thought, the more I wanted to know." I shrugged. "I didn't stop to consider my actions. I saw the opportunity and took it."

"Maybe that's another facet of control we need to concentrate on in your training."

I shuddered at the images and feelings. "I don't want this anymore. I don't want to hone it. I want to destroy it." Without having my hands on Miranda, I knew what she was thinking. I'd have this until the day I died—again.

"What did she show you?"

I frowned and shook my head. "I don't think it's something I can share, not even with you. It was not meant for me to see. I've stolen something from her, and I don't feel right about revealing it."

"Must've been bad then." Miranda took a step back. "She didn't kill anyone, did she?"

"Nothing like that." I held out my fist, and Miranda bumped it. I felt overwhelming curiosity tempered by a personal code of ethics, something I was obviously lacking.

For the drive home, I pulled out my iPod and picked the loudest, angriest music I had and cranked the volume as far as it would go. I counted the stops signs and street lights, anything to keep my mind occupied to block what I'd seen and felt. But when I lay down to sleep that night, they came.

I was in Jade's body seeing through her eyes, feeling what she felt, and I hated it probably as much as she did.

"I thought we had an understanding, Duane."

I couldn't see the man Jade was talking to; her gaze was fixed on the road ahead. She was scared, angry, and repulsed.

"I thought we did, too." His tone was flippant, dismissive, and whatever they were discussing gave him no pause. He continued to drive at the same high speed. The dark terrain flew by.

"I need this job."

"We're not employer or employee tonight, just two adults out to have a good time."

Jade turned her head sharply, giving me a view of him. He was nice-looking, and his arms were heavily muscled, accentuated by the sleeveless shirt he wore. Jade looked down at her gym clothes. She wasn't dressed for a night on the town, and she seriously doubted that Duane had dinner in mind. "You're supposed to be taking me home, not out."

"Let's have a few drinks and talk. We never get to do that at work." Agitation laced his words. This probably worked on a lot of young women entranced by his good looks. For some, special interest being paid by the boss could be a lucrative opportunity. Duane obviously wasn't used to being rebuffed, gentle as it was.

"I want you to turn around and take me home, please." Jade managed to stay calm, but I could hear and feel the desperation in the word "please."

"Are you gay?" he asked without slowing.

I felt Jade's hand grip the door handle. "I'm not...attracted to you, Duane, and I want to go home now." Panic started to rise in both of us. She turned and looked at the darkened houses flying by, trying to gauge how much damage she would incur if she tried to jump. If she opened the door, that might be enough to let him know she was serious. It might also distract and cause him to slow down enough for her to make a break. I felt her other hand move down and unclip the seat belt. When the alarm started to chime, she opened the door. Duane hit the brakes hard and swerved onto the shoulder of the road.

"Are you crazy?" he screamed, but Jade didn't look back. She was out of the car and halfway down in a ditch. I felt the mud sucking at her shoes.

"Accept this as my resignation." She moved farther away from the car. She heard the door slam and the engine rev, and Duane was gone without argument.

A tear streaked down her face. I felt her hand go up and wipe at it angrily. The thoughts that went through her mind like a tide were my own. *I'll have to move. I'm not dropping another penny into that rat trap car. I'll have to spend my savings on something else. Another town, another start. I'm the queen of starting over.* Prospects for her were dismal. The knowledge was part of her without it being an active thought. A high school dropout who only had one area of expertise. She'd have to find another gym. Maybe this time the boss would be decent.

It was well past one in the morning before I finally managed to go to sleep.

Chapter 5

Kaylie, the teenage girl who worked for me part time, was thrilled when I called her Friday night and offered the entire weekend. Normally, she'd come in half a day Saturday and Sunday, but I needed a break. She knew to call me if there were more customers than she could handle, but otherwise she'd leave me alone.

I defied the diet plan and skipped breakfast. With a cup of coffee in hand, I settled on the couch and stared out the window at life going by, thinking, and feeling sorry for myself. Actually, I felt sorry for everyone else, too. Up until recently, I thought about my own problems—no groceries, the power bill was much higher than it should've been, the light switch in the spare bedroom wasn't working, on and on and on. Insignificant stuff, but a burden nonetheless. Now I was privy to everyone else's problems and hurts, and they were so much bigger than mine… until now.

The sound of a key moving in the lock of my front door startled me. I was so absorbed in my own thoughts I didn't notice Miranda coming up the front walk. As always, she walked in like she owned the place and smiled at me.

"Good morning," she said cheerfully.

I grunted in response.

Miranda breezed past me into the kitchen. I could hear the clink of the coffeepot as it met with her cup. A spoon dropped onto the counter, then she was back. She took a seat in a chair opposite me with an expression imploring me to do more than grunt.

"I'm depressed." I took a sip of coffee that had grown cold and set the cup on the table in front of me.

"About?"

"Everyone I touch is sad. The woman with cancer, Jade and her troubles, you and…" I didn't bother to finish, she knew. "I feel like the whole world is suffering, but we go on hiding behind fake smiles."

Miranda was thoughtful for a minute. When in deep concentration, she rubbed the bridge of her nose with her index finger. I watched each stroke as she stared at my coffee cup. "I'm not sad," she said after a minute or two. "I'll admit I was deeply troubled after the incident with you, but now that we're talking about it, I'm probably not going to see the therapist anymore." She cocked her head. "I do replay your accident, but it doesn't affect me as much as it did."

I shrugged. "So?"

Miranda went back to rubbing the bridge of her nose. "You've burned yourself on the stove, right?"

I nodded.

"And every time you go into the kitchen, you remember that maybe just for a second. Pain is a powerful teacher and makes a lasting impression."

I thought about that for a second or two. "All my memories aren't painful. I have some really wonderful ones like the time Mom let us keep that kitten we found."

Miranda smiled. "I remember that, too." She began rubbing the bridge of her nose again and looked at me. "I think it's about timing. You touched me when I was grappling with your accident. You touched a woman who had just been told she was dying, and Jade, well, only you know that." She snapped her fingers. "You need to touch someone who is obviously happy."

"I'll touch you then. You said you aren't sad."

"No, no, we need a fresh candidate. Someone you don't share a past with." Miranda grinned. "Get dressed, we're going to the store."

My hair was still wet from my shower when we walked

through the back entrance to my store. Kaylie had the Windex out and was cleaning the glass counter at the register. She smiled brightly as we walked in. "Good morning," she said with exuberance.

"Been busy?" Miranda walked around the front of the counter.

"Only two browsers so far." Kaylie went back to scrubbing at a particularly thick smudge.

Miranda motioned with her eyes as I stood there trying to remember what I was there to do. I walked behind the counter. "I really appreciate you handling things for me." I laid my hand on Kaylie's shoulder.

Miranda must've said something, too, because in the distance I heard them talking while images flooded my mind. Kaylie had a calculator, and she was furiously punching in numbers. The total came to seven thousand four hundred dollars and some odd cents. I felt the sting in my hands as she clapped and bounced on her chair. She looked at the car on her computer screen. I felt the thrill coursing through her. A couple hundred more dollars, and it would be hers. In her mind, she was taking a ride down the coast, wind blowing in her blond hair, music blaring, her dog at her side. It filled her with such excitement that I could feel it bubbling up in my chest.

I felt the smile on my face when I stepped back and broke the connection. Miranda's eyes conveyed the excitement she felt. Another successful experiment, and she couldn't wait to hear the details.

"If you need anything at all, Kaylie, just call me. I'll be around the house for most of the day."

"Well, that's not exactly true." Miranda looked between us both. "Sparky has to go in for a checkup, and you know Marty won't go with me."

I folded my arms. "So that's why you suggested that I shower? Just so I could get Sparky stink all over me?"

"What's wrong with Sparky?" Kaylie asked.

"He doesn't like going to the vet," Miranda said.

"What's wrong with Sparky is he's sixty pounds of high anxiety to begin with, add in a trip to the vet, and that's compounded by a million." I dreaded the Sparky trips. Marty was a wise woman to refuse. "He won't go into the building. We have to pick him up and pry his paws off the doorjamb, then he shows his teeth to everyone and snaps at the doctor while they muzzle him."

"Oh." Kaylie looked like she was happy she didn't have to take part.

"So what happened with Kaylie?" Miranda asked.

I turned to look at her, but instead of meeting her blue eyes, I met brown, and the breath that buffeted my face was really awful. Miranda gave Sparky a gentle push, and he moved back to his spot at the window behind the driver's seat. He stuck his head out the half-opened window, and his tongue took to the breeze, slapping the side of his face and the glass, leaving trails of spittle.

"She's planning to buy a car, and she almost has enough money. I could feel her excitement so intensely." I sighed. "It was such a great feeling."

"I knew it was something happy by the look on your face." Miranda banged her fist on the steering wheel in time with the music on the radio. "It's timing. You can't let those first few experiences get you down. This has a high side."

High side. If there was one, I still wasn't seeing it. Yes, it was great to experience utter bliss through someone else, but therein lay the problem. Joy or not, I was still a voyeur, an unwilling participant. I wanted to touch and feel the warmth and softness of another's skin, not their lows or highs.

Miranda was trying to be upbeat for my sake. Determined to focus on the positive to work through this issue, so I could live life normally again. But for me, I knew normal wasn't going to be anything I recognized anymore. I felt myself slipping deeper into the abyss, a very lonely abyss.

A low growl came from the backseat as we turned into the vet's parking lot. I looked back at Sparky, and he looked at me like I was a traitor. "Sorry, boy. Just make the best of it, and it'll all be over soon." He didn't look so convinced. Actually, he looked like he wanted to gnaw my face off. I climbed from the car quickly.

Miranda had to crawl into the backseat to clip the leash on his collar because Sparky had wedged himself in the opposite corner of the back dash. "Come on, boy," Miranda said with a grunt as she tugged. Sparky managed to grab a little traction on the fabric of the seat, but Miranda, with brute strength alone, grabbed him by the collar and pulled him from the car. First hurdle crossed, the second would be more difficult.

We walked across the lot behind Sparky, who peed on everything he could get a leg over, a pleasant distraction for all of us, but then came the door, and hurdle two loomed above us. I opened it and stepped inside as Miranda picked up Sparky. All four paws went to the doorjamb. I'd get one paw down and move to the next, only to have the first paw wedge against the facing.

I was too busy to wonder how it would affect me to touch an animal. I tucked two paws into my armpit and grabbed for the other two while Miranda pushed. All the while, emotions ran through me without thought—nervousness, fear, anger, and confusion. It was at that moment that I wished this gift or curse or whatever it was worked two ways. I wanted to lay a hand on Sparky and make him understand it was all okay. Unfortunately, the transfer was only one-sided, and all the strokes and scratches left Sparky unaffected and me covered in stinky dog fur.

Miranda found a far corner of the room where she could stand and let Sparky pace. I checked in at the desk. The woman, obviously familiar with Sparky, grimaced. I took a seat and rested up for hurdle three—the door that led to the examining room. Dogs of all sorts on leashes shared the same dreadful look that Sparky did. Cats not so much. They mewled from kennels occasionally, a few on leashes themselves sat on their owner's laps, viewing the spectacle with wary indifference.

"What sort of breed is your dog?" the lady next to me asked.

I was quick to clarify. "He's not my dog. He belongs to my best friend. I just came along to help." I looked over at Sparky and wondered what he was. Some sort of shepherd maybe judging by the tufts of fur. Maybe some Irish setter with the red in his coat. I was stumped on the smashed-in snout. I turned and looked at the woman. "The jury is still out on that one. I suppose he's a mixture of just about everything. Possibly even donkey."

The woman nodded, seeming to accept my answer. She stroked the tiny black poodle in her lap that looked at the door to the back offices with dread. The poodle and I looked up when the exterior door opened. It took me a second to recognize Jade as she stepped into the room holding a haggard-looking cat in her arms. Her street clothes didn't detract from the magnificent body they covered. The yellow snug-fitting T-shirt showed off her arms while the colorful board shorts showed off a shapely pair of legs. Her hair hung freely down her back, and I marveled at the gloss of the rich brown tresses as she checked in with the desk clerk.

The clerk who spoke much louder than Jade explained that the cat would have to be in a kennel or on a leash. Apparently, Jade was unaware of this and accepted a leash that she awkwardly put around the cat's neck. She turned and faced the room, obviously uncomfortable with being the center of attention, and I thought maybe unfamiliar with being in a vet's office. I waved at her and watched as a slight look of relief crossed her face. She walked over and took the seat next to me.

"I didn't know you were a cat person," I said when she settled and stroked the cat that sat rigidly on her lap.

"I'm not, at least not until two days ago." She looked down at the ragged animal that was missing patches of fur. The tip of his right ear was gone, and there were deeply imbedded scratches on his nose. Fur black as coal hid whatever other injuries he might've had. "I found this guy in the parking lot of my building. I petted him once, and he seems to have adopted me." She looked at me oddly. "I've never had a pet before. I don't even know how to care for one."

The woman sitting across from us with a kennel in her lap spoke up. "Dr. Gary will probably be able to tell you how old he is and give him a first round of shots. You may want to consider having him neutered if he's not already. They tend to wander when they're not fixed," the woman lowered her voice, "and they spray."

Jade and I exchanged glances at the word "spray."

The woman cleared her throat. "They mark their territory by spraying urine on things, sort of like a dog does when he lifts a leg."

I nodded, and Jade looked disgusted.

I heard someone clear her throat and looked in Miranda's direction. She was miming something with her hands. I looked at her with brows raised, and she rolled her eyes and did the thing with her hand again. Finally, she said softly through her teeth, "toush er hat."

What? I mouthed.

"Touch her cat." Miranda hadn't meant to speak so loudly and turned dark red when everyone in the room turned to look at her.

It did sound odd, though I knew what she meant. "Pet the cat" would've made more sense.

I smiled at Jade meekly. "May I pet him?"

Jade waved at Miranda, noticing her for the first time, and said, "sure."

The fur felt a bit greasy to my hand. He'd probably taken refuge in the undercarriages of vehicles where Jade lived. Like my encounter with Sparky, I did not see images or hear thoughts, but I did have feelings wash over me that were similar to Sparky's—confusion, fear, and an odd curiosity. "He seems nice," I said, unable to think of anything else.

Miranda raised her brows and nodded slightly, wanting to know if I got anything. I shrugged and looked back at the people in the room. They were all watching with mystified expressions. As though Miranda nor I had ever encountered a cat and were discovering them for the first time.

I looked back at Jade. "How's your foot?"

She made a face. "Black and blue. The weight caught me right on the edge of my foot and pinched the skin. I guess I should be thankful that it didn't break anything, but it hurt," she lowered her voice, "like a bitch."

"Sparky Donahue."

"Oh, God." I stood and prepared myself for the battle. Upon hearing his name, Sparky began to recoil and tried to hide himself behind Miranda's legs. The leash was completely wrapped around her before I crossed the room. Miranda tried to walk in a circle to untie herself, but Sparky moved with her, undoing her progress.

Finally, she shimmied the leash down her legs like she was taking off a pair of pants.

Sparky was showing his teeth and flicking his tongue like a snake as she carried him toward the door, then came the paw plant. I didn't have time to get through the doorway first, so I ended up crawling beneath one of Sparky's legs. I could hear snickers and chuckles as the other pet owners watched the display. Again, we played the shell game with Sparky's paws—move one, then the other, go back to the first paw.

"Sometimes, it seems like he has forty legs," I said to the woman who tried to avoid Sparky's mouth and help with the paws. All the while, Miranda was grunting and pushing until we made it into the hall. Dr. Gary and another assistant were waiting with the muzzle, and that was another wrestling match.

When they took his temperature, Sparky let out a growl that clearly said he did not appreciate the violation. I stood off in the corner while the doctor and Miranda talked. Each sentence was punctuated by a growl as Sparky put in his two cents, which were probably profane.

Tests were run, and Sparky got a couple of shots that really pissed him off. Dr. Gary and his assistant left the room before Miranda removed the muzzle. Sparky was smart enough not to bite the hand that fed him, but that didn't apply to me. I kept a wary distance and followed slowly behind Miranda. When we walked back into the waiting room, Jade was at the counter. Miranda handed me her wallet and allowed Sparky to drag her out the door. I got in line behind Jade. "Everything go okay?" I nodded toward the cat.

"Yep, they think he's less than a year old. They ran some tests, and despite the exterior, he appears to be in good health." Jade scratched the cat behind his ears. "I made an appointment to have him neutered next week."

"What's his name?"

Jade looked at me for a moment, then back at the cat. "I don't know."

"Well, he looks like a tough guy to me. Maybe you should name him something like Spike or…Hellcat?"

Jade wrinkled her nose at my suggestion. "Tough guy," she said. "Guy, I like that. He'll be Guy."

I watched as she paid her bill, then she moved to the side as I paid Miranda's. I half expected her to dart off when the business was done, but she didn't. We walked out together, and I spotted Miranda off in the vacant lot next to the building where it appeared that Sparky was peeing on every single blade of grass.

"So how's the diet plan working out for you?" Jade asked as she walked slowly beside me.

"I went grocery shopping after you gave me the list, and I've even been experimenting with some of the recipes in the handout." I didn't bother to tell her that I skipped breakfast that morning and was operating on the sugar from my coffee alone.

"It's not easy to eat right. Too many quick and fattening alternatives at your fingertips, but if you'll stick to the plan, you'll have more energy to burn, and the workouts will be easier."

I glanced at Jade's well-defined arms. "You must be very disciplined. I don't know if I'll ever reach the level of fitness you've attained."

Jade shook her head, and for a moment, I thought she was agreeing that I'd never amount to much in the fitness department. "Don't use me as a gauge. Although I do work hard for the muscle I've built, what you see is false advertisement."

I almost stopped walking. "How can that be?"

"Genetics," Jade said simply. "My mother and father were both tall and slender, even though neither of them watched what they ate or exercised." Jade leaned against an old truck I assumed was hers. "We aren't all the same. People look at me and think if they eat perfectly and work hard enough that they'll have the same body. They'll feel better and be heathier, but not all will look like me." Jade cleared her throat. "That sounds arrogant, but I don't mean it that way. I was just…lucky, and I capitalize on that."

"That's…disappointing."

Jade chuckled, though her face showed no mirth. "If it'll make you feel any better, you have a good shape. You're not real tall, but you're above the average height. I figure about…five-eight?"

I nodded.

"You're not carrying a lot of extra weight. You'll tone nicely, and I think you'll be happy with the results." She looked out at Miranda. "She's going to have a more difficult time. Do you know if obesity runs in her family?"

"She never knew her father, but her mother was relatively heavy-set."

Jade looked back at me. "There's going to come a time when she sees the changes in you but doesn't see them in herself. That's going to be very discouraging. You're gonna have to be very supportive." Jade smiled in her odd way. "From what I've seen, you both seem to be very supportive of each other. I don't think that'll be a problem, but I did want to make you aware of what to expect."

Though she fake smiled when she mentioned being supportive, I felt that she envied the closeness between Miranda and me the way we envied her fitness. I didn't want to talk about workouts or diet anymore. I wanted to know about her. I wanted her to confide in me, so I could show her that same support I thought she wanted. It was an odd revelation. Aside from my friends, I realized that until recently, I really didn't care what other people felt. They had their own friends and family to be there for them, and I had mine. Jade was a virtual stranger, and I wanted to be…her friend.

"How'd you become a fitness guru?" I asked.

Jade rolled her eyes at my choice of words. "I wouldn't consider myself a guru." She opened the passenger's side door and laid the cat on the seat. Guy curled into a ball content to be out of her arms. She closed the door softly and leaned against the truck again. "My first job was at a fitness center. I mostly cleaned up tanning beds. I was a janitor, really. We were allowed to use the pool and the equipment after hours, and I liked to swim, so I always stayed behind. One of the trainers got me into weightlifting and exercise, and before long, my body started changing. My boss noticed and enrolled me in some fitness courses and a few nutrition classes. After that, I was promoted to trainer." Jade shrugged. "There was jealousy, and I heard a few of the trainers saying it was more about what I looked like than what I knew. One said I was a walking billboard, and that's why I was promoted."

I could hear the hurt in her voice when she talked. "But you didn't believe that, right?"

Jade averted her eyes. "Yes, I did." She looked back at me, her expression cold and stoic. "I've learned a lot, and I'm a great trainer, but what gets me the jobs are my looks. Would you train with someone with a gut or big thighs?"

She had a point. I needed to see the results of what the hard work could bring before I committed.

Jade went on without my answer. "When I interview, they really don't look at my experience. It's frustrating because I feel…" I could tell she hadn't meant to say as much as she did. Her face flushed, and she looked down at the keys in her hand.

"It's…important to me that you finish that sentence." I stuffed my hands into my pockets and clenched my fists, afraid that she wouldn't.

"Why?"

I blushed then. "Because I misjudged you, and it would put me in my place to hear the truth."

She looked at me with an expression that bordered on anger and surprise. "You thought I didn't have a care in the world. That I probably had my pick of suitors, maybe even the perfect partner waiting on me at home, didn't you?"

Mentally, I was acknowledging that she was right, but then it hit me. She'd dropped two bombs in what she said—she was single, and she used the word "partner." Straights didn't do that. She took my awkward smile as guilty agreement. "Finish the sentence, please."

Jade sighed. "I feel like a hooker, selling my body for money."

"I'm sorry." I held up my hand when she opened her mouth. "I'm sorry that you're made to feel that way, and I'm sorry that I judged you on your looks."

We fell silent after that. Me looking at her and her at me. I had no idea what swirled in her mind, but I wasn't about to touch her. To find out the truth might hurt, and I felt like I was hanging myself out there in the breeze. It was scary to reach out to someone. I suppose that's why I never did it. Friendship just happened to me. I'd never had to work for it, and I realized that I wanted this woman's favor.

"Do you forgive me?" I asked.

She considered my question for a moment, then softly said, "Why do you care?"

I didn't know how to answer. I stared at the ground and balled my fists tighter in my pocket. "I don't really know," I said honestly. "It's just…important for some reason that you forgive me."

"But you don't know if I judged you or not. What if I had a negative opinion of you? Would you forgive me?"

"Did you judge me?" I looked up at her.

"Yes, I thought you were…one of those women who used the gym as a pickup place. Not really interested in working out, just hanging around looking for fresh meat."

The statement stung as it slapped me between the eyes. Yes, I had gone in support of Miranda, but that's exactly what I was doing—just looking for the next woman to date and dump when things got too…intense. "And what is your opinion now?"

Jade looked off at the road. "That you're a lousy pickup artist because you haven't scored since I've been there, at least from what I noticed."

"Did you mean that to be as mean as it sounded?"

Jade shook her head and actually smiled, a real smile that showed all her teeth and crinkled her eyes. I marveled at the change in her countenance.

"That was a joke. And yes, I forgive you. Will you forgive me for thinking you were a player?"

"No, because you were partially right. I was cruising the gym."

Jade's eyes narrowed. "You said *was*. That means past tense. Have you met someone who has tamed you?" The fake smile was back.

"No…I…um…I died."

Jade's mouth twitched, and the right side of her lip rose slightly. When I didn't laugh, it became a thin line, and I could see wariness in her eyes.

"I guess it's considered a near-death experience. I was in West Virginia with friends, and I walked out onto a pond that I thought was frozen through." I shrugged. "I'm from Florida, I didn't know. Anyway, the ice broke, and it took them a while to get me out. From what Miranda and the others figure, I was dead for a little under twenty minutes."

"She talks about it casually, doesn't she?" Miranda said as she walked up. Sparky sniffed my legs, then moved to Jade's.

Jade looked at her and back at me. I shrugged again. "I guess I do sound causal about it. Maybe I'm still coping with the gravity of it all. It changed me, though."

I watched Jade swallow as her mind took it all in. "Well, I'm glad things turned out the way they did then," she said awkwardly.

"Me too," Miranda agreed. "We need to get Sparky home. I think he's pulled my shoulder out of socket."

Jade took that as her cue. "It was nice talking to you. I'll see y'all at the gym," she said with a wave and climbed into her truck.

Once we had Sparky loaded up and we were on the road, Miranda glanced over at me. "You've got a lot to tell, so start talking."

Chapter 6

Thunder woke me Sunday morning. I flicked on the TV in my bedroom and watched the local weather for a few minutes before trying to call Kaylie. It went straight to voice mail where I left her a message saying she didn't have to come in, business would be slow anyway. I asked her to call me when she got the message. She did five minutes later from the store phone. Since she was already there, the day was hers.

For breakfast, I had something low in sugar and high in fiber and a cup of coffee. I lay around watching TV until almost noon. For lunch, I made turkey on wheat sandwiches and took one to Kaylie so she wouldn't have to go out in the weather.

Kaylie had swept and mopped the entire store; it smelled of disinfectant when I walked in. She'd also used the quiet time to rearrange the stockroom. I whistled when I saw all that she'd accomplished. "You rock, Kaylie," I said with a smile.

She blushed at the praise. "I figured while I was here, I should at least be doing something." Her eyes widened when she spied the sandwiches on the counter. "Is one of those mine?"

"Yep. I hope you like Sun Chips, I'm on a health kick." I supposed she did because she'd already plugged two into her mouth before I got to the counter. "You've worked for me for two years, haven't you?"

She nodded and her ponytail flopped against the back of her neck.

"You've come in anytime I asked, and you always do a great job. I think that deserves a bonus." I couldn't help but smile. She'd stopped chewing, and her cheeks were bulging.

Kaylie swallowed with a gulp. "Thank you!"

"What are you gonna do with the extra bucks?" I could tell she wanted to ask how much it was going to be but was too polite.

"I'm saving to buy a car, so the extra money will go into that fund."

"Have you factored in insurance?"

"Yes, ma'am."

"How much are you lacking in your fund?"

"Around two hundred dollars."

I knew she'd answered honestly because I'd seen her figures when I touched her the day before. "So five hundred dollars would get the car, insurance, gas, and perhaps an outside mechanic's opinion that the car is a good buy?"

Kaylie's eyes went round behind her sandwich. "Yes, ma'am," she said slowly.

"Then surprise, that's how much your bonus is." She came around the counter screaming with bits of sandwich flying out of her mouth and jumped on me before I could stop her. My mind went to hers before I could even think to stop it.

The day was sunny, and I could hear the streamers above my head flapping in the breeze, cheesy eye catchers that used car salesmen circled their lots with to draw attention. The VW Bug had a few scratches and dents, but the upholstery looked good, and besides it was blue, Kaylie's favorite color. I could hear her praying in my head, *Please, God, don't let anyone buy it before I can.* I felt the warmth of the hood when she put her hand on it and spoke. "You're mine. I'll be back for you soon."

"Are you okay?" She was looking at me, concern etched her brow.

"I'm fine, got a little choked on a chip during the excitement." I cleared my throat for effect. "Would you like me to go ahead and pay you today?"

She looked like she was going to cry. "Yes, ma'am, that would be great."

"Then I'll do it on two conditions." Her brows rose as she nodded, agreeing to whatever I had to say before it came out of my mouth. "Stop calling me ma'am, it makes me feel old, and promise that you'll take the car to a mechanic before you hand over the money."

"I will. My dad knows someone." She clapped her hands and squealed.

"Will your dad go with you to buy the car?"

"Yes, ma—yes, he will. I have three sisters, and we all have to buy our own first cars. Dad says we'll take care of them if we have to buy them ourselves. He's kind of strict about money, but he always goes when one of us picks one and helps with the buying."

She looked like she was going to hug me again, and I slipped off the stool and grabbed my sandwich. "I'm gonna go back to my office and make out the check."

"Okay," she said with a beaming smile. "Thank you so much, Sloan."

Maybe she couldn't sit still or she was determined to show her appreciation, but that child had scrubbed half the windows in the store until they were crystal clear by the time I returned. "I need to go back to the house, so I'm leaving the check right here on the counter," I called out to her. "Put it in your purse as soon as you can. The windows look great, thanks."

I was happy to share in her joy and receive her hugs, but I felt wrong for allowing her to touch me without knowing what I could do. Besides, Miranda and I had already used her as an experiment, and I felt guilty enough about that.

I flopped back down on the couch and surfed the channels looking for something to get into. My phone rang a few minutes into a Lifetime movie. I grabbed it up, expecting it to be Miranda, but I didn't recognize the number. Prepared to tongue lash a phone solicitor, I answered.

"Uh, Sloan?"

"Yes," I said, trying to place the voice.

"This is Jade from the gym."

I thought it kind of amusing that she felt she had to clarify who she was as if there were a million Jades running around Panacea. "Hey, Jade, what's up?"

"It's…uh…crappy outside, and I wanted to go see a movie. I…don't want to go alone. Would you be interested?"

"Sure. What do you want to see and what time does it start?"

"I don't care, and I have no idea." She chuckled.

"Okay, do you want to meet me here and we'll look on the computer or do you want me to pick you up and we'll look at yours? There are a couple of theaters in Tallahassee, so we have choices."

"I'm at the gym. If you want to meet me here, we can look online, then head out."

"Give me about forty-five minutes to grab a shower and get over there."

"Okay, see you then."

I jumped off the couch and ran into the bathroom. I showered and dressed and was out the door in record time. It wasn't until I was behind the wheel that I thought about what I was doing. I hated movie theaters. There was never anything that I wanted to see bad enough that I couldn't wait for it to come out on video. I was spoiled by my DVD player. I could lie down in my favorite ragged clothes and pause the movie when I wanted to go to the bathroom. Nevertheless, I was going out on a stormy day to sit in a crowded theater to watch…something.

It was Jade. I wanted to be with her, perhaps for different reasons than two months earlier. But now, I was simply intrigued with another human being, and I wanted to get to know her. At least that's what I told myself. Truth be known, she was attractive and I was attracted, but there wasn't anything I could do about it. It wasn't a date anyway. She was reaching out in friendship, and I was willing to take it.

After I arrived at the gym, I walked down the hall to the last office, a closet really, and found Jade staring at a laptop. She spun it around to face me. "Comedy, romance, and thrillers. What's your pick?"

I looked at the choices and noticed a comedy that I'd seen the trailer for. "How about something funny?"

"Fine by me. When does it start?"

I looked at my watch. "At four. I think we can make it if you let me drive." I grinned when Jade cocked her head. "I know all the shortcuts, and I'm a shitty navigator."

"I guess you're driving then."

Jade had to adjust the seat before she could even climb into my Mustang. When I looked over at her, she appeared to be riding in the backseat her head was so far back. "This car isn't much for leg room, is it?" I said apologetically.

"This car is *fine*." Jade leaned over, looking at all the gauges and nearly brushed against me. I froze, hoping we wouldn't make contact. The thought occurred to me that if she casually touched my arm or brushed my hand while I was driving, there was no telling where we'd end up. I slumped against the door, hoping she'd think I was doing it to look cool.

"I take it you like Mustangs."

"I like muscle cars." Jade looked around the backseat, which she was presently sitting in. "I really like this retro look."

"What kind of car do you have?"

"A shitty truck."

"That's foreign, right?"

Jade chuckled at my joke. "American, a Ford."

"I remember you leaned against it at the vet's office. Must be a lot easier for you to get in and out of. You mind if I ask how tall you are?"

"Six-foot-two. I wish I was your height, though. Buying clothes when you're a giant is a pain in the ass."

"Are you from Florida originally?" I asked, picking up on a slight accent.

"I grew up in Boise, Idaho, but I've lived a lot of places. I like the climate here. I might make this home."

"Are you an Army brat?"

"No." Jade looked out her window, and I took that as a sign that I was heading into something she didn't want to talk about. "What was it like?" she asked suddenly.

"What?"

She glanced my way, then looked out at the road. "Your experience…if you don't mind me asking."

"I didn't see anything if that's what you want to know. If I did, I don't remember it. Sort of like when you wake up after a deep sleep, you know you dreamed, but nothing comes to mind." I tapped the wheel with my finger. "No one seems to believe me. They all think I won't talk about it."

"You keep things to yourself a lot?"

I shrugged and exhaled loudly. "I tell Miranda pretty much everything but not the rest of my friends. They all talk freely about things that concern them, but I keep my thoughts to myself. I suppose I'm sort of private in that regard."

"Makes sense." Jade looked back out her window again. "Would I be invading your privacy if I asked you how the accident changed you? You don't have to answer if it's too personal, but ever since you told me, I've been curious."

I would've been curious, too. I had been about her. So much so that I touched her and invaded her privacy, but I couldn't be totally honest. Maybe one day I would, but not until I had it all sorted out in my mind and under some semblance of control. "There are some parts I can't discuss, parts that are still a bit raw and I need time to…cope with them before I can put them to words. The experience has made me look at life differently. I thought this was all there is, and even though I didn't see a tunnel of light or stunning visions, I came back with a knowing that this isn't our only existence."

I could see Jade looking at me out of the corner of my eye, her expression blank. She didn't say a word. It made me nervous.

I exhaled and continued. "I came back wanting…things."

"Like what?" she asked softly.

I regretted my admission, but something inside me said if I wasn't honest with her on this part, all would be lost. I wasn't really sure what that meant. "I've never been an affectionate person, but now…I crave it. I occupied my time with lots of women, but I felt nothing for them. When it became apparent that they were getting attached, I dropped them and ran the other direction. I want to be connected, and I'm not talking about sex. I want interaction, a connection with people."

"So you were really a player." Jade folded her arms. "Were

you playing the field until you found someone who you wanted to settle with, or was it just the thrill of the hunt?"

"No." I bit my lip, wishing that we were already in the theater where conversation wasn't necessary. "Fear of getting hurt. Fear of being happy and having it taken away." I couldn't believe I'd admitted that to her. There was only one person to whom I bared my soul because Miranda often knew me better than I knew myself. Maybe it was because I sensed Jade's hurt and how it permeated her being. Maybe I knew she'd understand.

"I see couples all the time, and I wonder how they make it work, especially the elderly ones that have been together forever. I wonder if it's truly love or if they just need each other so much that they can't make it on their own."

"Maybe a little of both. They love so intensely that they can't be apart."

"Scary, isn't it?" She said it so quietly I almost didn't hear her.

I pulled into the parking lot and killed the engine. "Yes, it is."

I'd heard Jade chuckle, but I'd never heard her release a full-blown laugh. She was slumped down in her seat, body-shaking, cackle laughing. I think I laughed at her more than I did the movie. As we sat there, I realized that maybe I was seeing something few others rarely or if ever did.

She shifted in her seat a lot, even though she was sitting on the end of the row, trying to accommodate her legs. Shorter than her, I was wiggling, too, then her leg connected with mine. Images more vivid than the movie played before my eyes, and I couldn't pull away.

I felt a breeze on my bare skin, the warmth of the sheets draped across my legs, the cool of the headboard against my back. A woman covered her breasts with her bra and reached for her shirt. "Why have I never seen your house?" I asked and heard Jade's voice speaking the words.

Blue eyes looked up at us. "You know it's complicated. My ex likes to makes things difficult for me. She drops in unannounced. She'd go crazy if she found you there."

Jade knew it was a lie. She'd known for a while, but she hoped things would change. They were having an affair. And for a time, Jade assuaged her conscience by allowing herself to accept the lie. "Lauren, is there ever going to be a time when we do things like normal couples do? Have dinner at home, watch a movie?"

Lauren smiled. "You'd rather do that instead of what we spent half the day doing?"

Jade was weary, I could feel it. "I guess what I'm asking is, will we ever really be together? Where's this relationship going?"

"Don't put pressure on me," Lauren said pleadingly. "I'm dealing with a lot at work, and my ex is driving me crazy. I can't make any long-term plans right now." Jade watched as she gathered her things. "I'll call you." The sound of her heels clacked across the floor, then a door closed.

Jade sighed deep and wearily. Lauren would call when she was ready for a tryst, but Jade wouldn't answer.

Jade shifted, and I blinked as the movie screen filled my eyes again. I felt used and angrier with myself than Lauren—Jade's feelings clung to me like a damp coat. I couldn't laugh anymore at the onscreen antics. Pivoting in my seat, I sat with my back nearly turned to her, avoiding contact. She took that opportunity to use the armrest, and no matter how much I squeezed into the other side of my chair, we came in contact.

I was being kissed roughly. The woman on top of Jade was grinding into her so hard it felt like my spine was being crushed into the hardwood floor where they were lying. Jade broke the kiss, and we gasped. "Stop," she said breathlessly.

The woman, who had moved to her neck and was showering it with bites and kisses, rose up on her arms and looked deep into my eyes. "Why?"

Jade didn't say anything as she stared into the pools of brown, myriad thoughts swirled in her brain. My mind swam as my brain scrambled to make sense of them all. I heard a familiar male voice say somewhere in Jade's mind, "Chloe and her friends are in stiff competition to see who will bed her first." I heard and felt Jade wish that she'd never overheard that conversation. I felt her desire for companionship and the sad realization that these brief interludes were all she was ever going to get, all she was worthy of.

"Let's move to the bed, the floor is killing me."

Chloe stood and gave Jade a hand up. I could feel the self-loathing, the sadness that permeated Jade. Arousal would be slow in coming. She hoped that Chloe wouldn't notice.

Jade moved again and broke the connection, and something wet hit my arm. My hand rose slowly to my face. It was damp from my tears. I choked back a sob and clamped my eyes shut until I regained my composure. The images and the accompanying feelings were so much more vivid, more intense than anything I'd experienced in prior encounters. When I looked back up at the movie screen, it looked dull in comparison.

I mustered the courage and looked at Jade. She was no longer laughing at the movie. Slumped down in her seat, she was staring down, not looking at the screen. A finger was pressed to her temple, and I could tell she was somewhere else, deep in thought. She's dwelling on these memories right now, I thought. That's why they were so intense. In her profile, I saw what I'd felt— sadness, deep unrelenting sadness.

There we sat two peas in a pod. I was too scared to let go and love, and Jade felt too unworthy to be loved. Had true love slapped either of us in the face, we'd never recognize it because both of us were incapable of receiving.

When the movie ended, we got up and merged into the crowd. In the foyer of the theater, I caught a glimpse of my reflection in the glass frame of a movie poster. I looked like hell. No one would've guessed that I'd just seen a comedy. My eyes were swollen, and my face looked puffy and fatigued.

Jade, who was ahead of me, stopped and waited. I caught the quick widening of her eyes when she looked at my face. She opened the door and held it for me to pass through. I mumbled a "thanks" and kept walking. She moved alongside me, and we walked silently to the car.

"You okay?" she asked once we were inside.

"Fine." A lie passed through my head, and I started to claim that I had an allergic reaction to strong perfume. Two months earlier, I might've let it roll off my tongue, but the urge to be honest with her overwhelmed me. I felt my eyes begin to burn again.

"Hey."

From the corner of my eye, I saw her hand move toward me. I recoiled, rolling my shoulders toward the door. Jade jerked her hand away.

"I know you have a germ phobia, but do you consider me that dirty?"

The latter part of the question was so heavily laced with emotion that I was immediately furious with myself. "No, no, I don't think you're dirty." I took a deep labored breath. "I've got a lot on my mind. I'm dealing with things that…tear me up inside. If you touch me, all the emotion is going to come tumbling out like a tidal wave, and I won't stop for what I fear may be days."

She was quiet as I turned the engine and pulled out of the parking lot. I had planned to ask her if she'd like to have dinner, but I needed to get her back to her car, then lock myself away. I wanted to take her in my arms and tell her that she was worthy, deserving of love and of happiness. But I couldn't, and for the first time in my life, I felt like it truly mattered.

"It's okay to cry, you know," she said after we'd ridden for a few minutes. "You can lean on me."

Jade didn't ask me what was wrong. She was simply offering comfort. Again, I felt my anger rise at myself, at whomever or whatever had laid this affliction upon me. Maybe I was being cosmically repaid for the hearts I'd broken in my selfish pursuits, but this punishment was too severe. I wasn't the only jacked-up soul out there who toyed with the emotions of others. At least, my reasons for doing so were because of fear and vulnerabilities. There were many who did it for sport, amusement.

"Would you like me to tell you something funny? It might take your mind off things for a little while."

I glanced over at her and smiled. "Yeah, I'd like that."

"Last night, Guy jumped up on the bed, right in the center of my chest." She looked over at me. "You ever wake up and not know where you are, even though you're in your own bed?"

"Many times, yes."

"I was sleeping so deep, and when that cat hit me, I forgot I had one. I sat straight up and screamed at the top of my lungs." She started laughing. "Poor Guy looked just like a cartoon character. He jumped straight into the air, all four paws spread eagle, and he screamed just as loud as I did and higher pitched."

The laugh rumbled up through me. The mental picture, though funny, wasn't truly the catalyst. I wanted to laugh at something. It felt good to release the pressure that had been building inside.

"After I calmed down, I went looking for Guy. I felt sorry for him. I have high ceilings in the kitchen, so there's sort of a roost on top of my cabinets, and he was up there hiding."

"You scared the shit out him, no doubt," I said with a laugh.

"I checked my bed for just that. I think the scare might've taken one or two of his nine lives."

I glanced in her direction. "Thanks for that. It helped a lot."

Jade nodded. "Sometimes, we just need something to laugh at."

She wasn't joking about her truck being shitty. The parking lot when I picked her up was full, but by the time we got back to the gym, her old Ford was the only thing out there. I figured it rolled off the assembly line in the early nineties. The door creaked loudly when she opened it. It cranked on the first try, though, and I followed her out of the parking lot in a billow of black smoke.

Later as I lay in bed, thoughts of Jade filled my mind. Two months before, I would've been hot on her trail, using every charm I had to get her into my bed. I didn't know how anyone could look at her and not be attracted. She had it all—a beautiful face, lovely hair, and a body that was eye-popping hot. Had I not peeked into her soul per se, I wouldn't have ever known that she was so self-deprecating. She carried herself with a confidence that belied what was going on inside. But now I knew she was just a tender soul wanting acceptance and love like the rest of us—like me.

I guess no one ever bothered to look past the armor, maybe Jade never let them. Perhaps she wouldn't have let me, but I'd gotten a glimpse of what and who she was. To me, that made her lovelier than what was on the outside. I looked at her with different eyes when she got into her truck that night. She was the total package and had no clue.

Chapter 7

"You did what?" Miranda stood on the other side of the counter with her hands on her hips.

"It was platonic. She didn't want to go to the movies alone."

"Until you get a handle on this thing, you're just tempting fate by making new friends." Miranda narrowed her eyes. "Don't stand there and tell me that you wouldn't jump P.P. if she gave you half a chance."

I started to fuss about the use of the nickname but decided that it was correct. Jade was perfection personified, at least in my eyes. "Have you forgotten? I can't jump anyone."

Miranda shook her head. "I haven't forgotten, but I wonder if sometimes you have. There's a mutual attraction there, Sloan. Right now, she might like you a little bit. If you continue to spend time with her, she may decide that she likes you a lot. Then what will you do?"

I had no answer. "I don't know. I'm just living one day to the next without a plan," I said testily.

Miranda softened her tone. "I worry for you both. I don't know her well at all, but I don't want to see either of you hurt."

"Me either."

"So let's analyze this." Miranda came behind the counter and took a seat on the stool next to me.

"I don't want to be analyzed."

Miranda sat quietly until I looked at her. "I know you don't, but I think you need to. Unfortunately, you can't live day to day anymore. You have to think ahead. So be honest and tell me how you feel about her."

I chewed the bottom of my lip as I swung my feet back and forth. "I don't lust after her. I don't spend my time trying to think of ways to seduce her. I just enjoy her company. She's really an extraordinary person. The more I learn about her, the more I want to know."

"Shit," Miranda said softly.

"What?"

"Let me ask you something." Miranda cocked her head to the side. "When you first met Paige, did you feel the same about her?" She held her hand up to forestall my answer. "Think about this for a minute."

Lonna's girlfriend was the newest addition to the group. When we first met, I was naturally curious about her, but with Jade…it felt completely different. "Shit. I'm just drawn to her I can't explain why."

Miranda shook her head sadly. "You've never been in love. You don't know how it feels to stand on the precipice right before the fall. That's where you're at."

"It's too soon, don't you think?" I asked, holding out hope and knowing what she said was true.

"There's no timetable." Miranda looked down at her shoes. "You need more time with your gift before you go any further with her. You need to back away."

"Gift! This isn't a gift. It's a penance! A blight." I hopped off the stool, and it clattered to the floor. "A gift is something you can use, something that's good to receive." I rounded the counter and kicked at the wall. Miranda let me huff and puff until I regained control.

"This is going to sound trite," she said forcefully. "But if you keep looking at it that way, that's all it's going to be. Quit running from something that is obviously a part of you and grab it by the balls. Learn to use it. Master it, make it work for you instead of against you."

"Okay, balls? Ew."

Miranda grinned and pointed at me. "Don't try to make me laugh. You know I'm right. If Mom were here, she would've already jerked some sense into you."

She was right. Momma Donahue would've popped me upside the head. "Give me time to adjust."

"No. You'll just talk yourself into circles like you've been doing the past two months. You're gonna get back into normal routines. You're gonna stop avoiding our friends. Tonight, Marty's boiling shrimp, and everybody's coming. You're coming, too."

I shook my head. "What if one of them touches me?"

"You didn't ask yourself that when you went out with Jade, and you won't use that as an excuse with me. The probability that you will be touched is high. I'll be right there with you. Try, Sloan, try hard to control it."

"Control it, right."

Miranda hung around the store until I closed. I was certain she did it to make sure I wouldn't back out. When we walked in, I could see Marty on the patio dropping the seasoning into the boiler. Her blond hair was in a ponytail, but the loose pieces were already curling from the steam rising out of the pot. Miranda and I were like stomping bulls, Marty was all poise and grace. She looked up when she heard us banging around in the kitchen while mixing drinks and waved.

"I told her not to hug you," Miranda said softly. "Actually, I told them all not to hug you. They think you're an emotional basket case right now, and the least bit of affection will make you cry, and we all know how you hate to do that."

"Well, thanks." I rolled my eyes.

"You had a better idea?" Miranda put her hands on her hips and looked at me.

"No, fresh out."

"Well, hey stranger." Deb walked into the kitchen. Neither Miranda nor I heard her and Angel come in. Deb looked at me with a wide smile. "You've lost weight. You look good."

I'd just started my diet and exercise program, and I knew for a fact that I'd gained two pounds since the last time I'd seen her, but I took the compliment anyway. Unlike me, Deb had lost weight. Her wedge hairstyle ran along her jawline accentuating how sharp it had actually become. She'd lightened her brown hair a shade, which made the shadows beneath her eyes look darker. I looked around to see if anyone else was affected by the change in Deb's appearance, but no one seemed to be as taken aback as I was. Then again, they'd seen her more often than I had and perhaps for them the change had been gradual.

Angel's blond braided ponytail flopped over her shoulder as she grabbed a beer from the fridge and offered one to Deb who waved her off and grabbed a bottle of water instead. Angel's blue eyes twinkled as she took a swig of her beer and asked, "How are the workouts going?"

"A nightmare from which there is no escape." Miranda tapped her glass with mine.

Angel and Deb laughed. "Miranda told us that a trainer from hell has written up a program for you to follow," Deb said. "She sounds like Attila the Hun in spandex."

"There are days when I would agree," I said with a laugh.

Marty walked into the kitchen and looped an arm around Miranda's shoulders. "As soon as Lonna and Paige get here, I'll put the shrimp on to boil. They're both coming straight from work, so it shouldn't be long." Marty turned her attention to me. "What've you been doing with yourself lately?"

"Working and working out, that's just about it." I pulled a necklace from my pocket. "This is for you to replace the one you lost on vacation." A small brightly colored shell was fastened in the middle, and I'd braided the brown leather strap on either side.

"Oh, it's beautiful." Marty's eyes twinkled as she took it from my hand. I was thankful that we didn't come in contact because whatever I saw, Miranda would demand to know.

"I'll put it on." Miranda took it from Marty and fastened it around her neck.

"The length is perfect." Marty pressed her fingers to it and smiled. "Thank you, Sloan."

"You're very welcome. I'm glad you like it."

"We're here. Please don't say you started without us," Lonna yelled as she came through the front door. Seconds later, she and Paige came bounding into the kitchen. Lonna laid a hand on her sidearm. "I'll shoot anyone that took the first potato. I'm sworn to protect, but I draw the line at the spuds."

Marty held her hands up. "Chill, Barney Fife, I haven't even put the shrimp on to boil, but now that you're here, I'll get it started."

"Hey, Sloan, good to see ya," Lonna said with a wave.

Paige, the quiet one of the two, waved, as well. "Hey, Sloan."

"Good to see y'all, too." I waved and felt stupid. They had the kid gloves on and were all gathered on one side of the bar, obviously keeping their distance like I was a leper.

"Let's go out to the patio," Miranda said. "It's cool tonight."

Everyone grabbed her drinks and headed for the back door. I thought I was bringing up the rear, but someone put a hand on my shoulder. I was in a jewelry store looking at a ring, excitement coursed through me. My heart swelled with love for Paige, and I couldn't wait to slip that ring on her finger and ask her to be mine until death do us part.

The connection broke. I had staggered in my haze and landed against the doorjamb.

"You okay?" Lonna put a hand to my arm, and I was off again. I was taking the ring out of a hiding place. It sparkled when I opened the box, and I felt a thrill pass through me. The credit limit on my card was blown, but it was worth every penny of interest that I'd pay.

I blinked, and Lonna, who was a head taller than me, was sporting an amused grin. "You're still clumsy, aren't you?"

I laughed, high off her joy. "Yes, I'm afraid that will never change." I stopped short of saying congratulations. When I walked onto the patio, I took a close look at Paige's hand. The ring wasn't there, the proposal hadn't been made.

"So what's everybody doing this weekend?" Deb asked. "I was thinking it would be fun to go to the beach and have a cookout."

"Miranda's off, aren't you, baby?" Marty asked.

Miranda nodded and looked at me. "Think you can get Kaylie to work this Saturday, too?"

"I don't know. I'll have to ask," I said as I took a seat. Sparky ran up to me and said hello; apparently, my assistance in the vet trip was forgotten.

"We won't be here." Lonna came to stand behind Paige's chair.

"We won't?" Paige looked surprised as she looked up at Lonna.

"No, love, we're going to Provincetown." Lonna laughed when Paige jumped into her arms. "It's a surprise," Lonna said with love in her eyes as she stroked Paige's blond hair. "I know you've always wanted to go. It'll only be for four days, though."

I wanted to feel sorry for myself while I sat there watching them wrapped in each other's arms. They looked at one another as though they'd forgotten we were gathered around them. I wanted to know what it was like to be totally captivated and adored.

"How cool," Angel said with a smile. "Take tons of pictures."

Paige turned around in Lonna's embrace. Her face was radiant, totally unaware that she would return from Provincetown a married woman.

I ate shrimp until I felt I would burst. When I finally quit, I leaned back in my chair, feeling bloated and tired. Everyone else appeared to feel the same. We all looked at one another and started laughing.

"Why do we do this to ourselves?" Lonna asked with a groan. She shot Paige a sideways glance. "And why didn't someone stop me when I got to the fourth potato?"

"I guess we failed on the moderation portion of our diet." Miranda tossed her napkin onto the table. "Jade's gonna take one look at us tomorrow night and know that we gorged ourselves. She's not even our trainer, and she can make me feel like a worm if I'm not giving a hundred percent."

"Oh, yes, the dominatrix." Lonna grinned. "We've heard all about her. One of the guys in the department trains with her, and he says she's a royal bitch."

The compulsion to defend Jade rose up within me, but before I could utter a word, Miranda jumped in. "Not really," she said as she draped an arm over the back of Marty's chair. "She's no-nonsense, and she makes you give the workout your all. She does exactly what a trainer is supposed to do, and that's precisely why Sloan and I *don't* train with her."

"Bullshit," Lonna said with a grin. "Her client list is booked. The minute she walked onto the floor of that gym, her ticket was filled. She's hot, and everybody wants their time with her. It doesn't have anything to do with her skill."

Lonna reaffirmed everything Jade had said that day at the vet's office. She was smart to capitalize on her looks, but it had to be disheartening that people considered her a bitch for doing what she was being paid to do. I shook my head in disgust. "It just harkens back to what women have been saying for years. If you're strong and competent, you're a bitch, but if you're a man, you're just tough."

"That's why I don't mind being called a bitch," Deb said. "Of course, if they make the mistake of saying it to my face, I show them what a bitch I can really be."

Lonna shook her head. "It pisses me off regardless of the connotation. I don't see it as a compliment in any form. I don't even like it when someone is just playing. I feel like they're saying, 'You're tough and strong, but you're really just a grumpy woman.' But I work with mostly men, so I'm more sensitive to it, I guess."

I wanted no part of that particular thread of conversation; it made my blood boil. And I was tired of the smell of shrimp on my hands. I stood and rolled up the newspaper with the shrimp shells and took it to the trash. I found a lemon in the kitchen and began scrubbing my hands with it to get the smell out of my skin. Deb walked in, and I gave her a slight smile as she did the same.

"You doin' all right, Sloan?" she asked as she came to stand beside me at the sink.

"I'm fine—" Deb's leg rested against mine as we scrubbed, and she took the lemon from my hand.

I was standing in front of a full-length mirror looking at Deb's refection. She turned sideways and ran her hand over a flat stomach. I felt her pleasure at feeling and seeing her new body.

Someone at work described her as "skinny," and she was thrilled. I wanted to close my eyes as she began pulling off her top to try on another, but I couldn't. Deb was still looking at herself in the mirror. Her ribs were showing, and even her sternum stood out starkly.

Just a few more pounds went through her mind and mine. We heard movement from somewhere in the house, and she quickly pulled on another top. Angel had been furious with her when she found all the laxatives. Puking wasn't her favorite thing to do, but she'd gotten pretty good at it. She could do it quietly now as long as she kept the bathroom door locked. *Just a few more pounds.*

I was shaking when Deb moved to dry her hands. I glanced over at her and noticed for the first time the clothes she was wearing. She'd been heavy as long as I'd known her. She always wore things that were loose to hide her weight. She was still doing the same thing, but this time, she was hiding her lack of weight.

"You stuffed?" Miranda asked as she walked into the kitchen.

"Yeah," I said shakily. "And I'm tired. I think I'm gonna call it a night."

"I'll come by in the morning. I don't have to work again until Wednesday." Miranda picked up a slice of lemon and began rubbing her hands with it. "You okay?"

Deb turned and looked at me. I smiled at her, then looked back at Miranda. "Fine."

Miranda walked me to the back door where I did my stupid wave thing and said good night to everyone. Then she followed me out to the car. "You have a really strange look on your face." She leaned down, looking at me through my window.

"I saw things tonight." I looked up into her blue eyes and debated on what I should admit.

"You're torn about what you should tell me."

I nodded.

"Well, you're gonna have to weigh it like this—will it benefit anyone I know what ypu know? Because I understand about not wanting to invade anyone's privacy. I expect you to respect mine, so I guess I should respect that of others."

"Let me sleep on it."

"All right." Miranda stepped back, and I pulled out of her driveway.

I really didn't think I was going to sleep at all. Loud music and counting on the drive home failed me. The thoughts came, and I had no choice but to dwell on them.

Chapter 8

"She's happy."

"But she's killing herself, Sloan." Miranda tapped her fingers on the counter. "Angel told me not to compliment Deb on her weight loss anymore. I tried to ask her why, but Deb walked in and she bottled up."

"This has really bolstered her self-confidence. How are we gonna confront this without alienating or crushing her?"

Miranda folded her arms. "Deb is so freaking bullheaded. She isn't going to take lightly anything we have to say. Angel is obviously aware of the problem because of what she said, but I doubt she knows how to handle it."

"That makes three of us."

"She was really bony?" Miranda asked.

"Yeah. From what was going through her head, Angel had found the laxatives she's been taking. She's gonna make herself throw up from now on."

"Jeez, I wanna lose weight, but I'd never go to that extreme." Miranda pointed at me. "I bet this started when that guy at work called her a lard ass. She was really bunged up about that. If that's the case, she's been doing this for a while."

"Should we talk to Angel? Maybe tell her that we've noticed Deb has really gotten too skinny."

Miranda came around the counter and sat down. "She looked so good when we went on vacation. I bet we made it worse when we went on about how much she'd lost." Miranda rubbed the bridge of her nose for a moment. "Yeah, we should probably talk to Angel."

I'd suggested it, but I didn't like the idea. If Angel went into protective mode, we'd have an even bigger battle ahead. "What if we just went to Deb? We've been friends a long time, maybe she'd hear us out."

In hindsight, we should've stuck to plan A. Miranda and I tried the gentle approach and told Deb that we thought she looked wonderful but maybe she was taking it too far. First, she glibly denied that she was underweight, but Miranda pushed and wanted to know how she was continuing to lose.

"I diet. I watch everything I eat. I count the calories before anything goes into my mouth." Deb looked at us, and I could tell she was getting pissed.

"How much do you weigh now?" Miranda said. "If you don't mind my asking."

Deb's lips turned up in what she obviously hoped was a smile but looked more like a sneer. "I do mind, that's a rude question."

"We're friends, Deb. Sloan and I are on diets, too. I'd have no problems telling you how much I weighed if I lost a few pounds."

"If we were having a casual conversation, I suppose I wouldn't mind. But you two come to my house uninvited and start asking specific questions about my diet and weight. I find that strange."

"We're just concerned," I said. "You seem to be losing an awful lot, and we wanted to make sure you weren't sick."

"I'm not sick," Deb said defensively.

"Good, that takes a load off my mind." I smiled, but Deb didn't return it.

"You looked at me so strangely in the kitchen the other night. What was that all about?" Deb asked, raising a brow.

"I noticed how thin your arm was when you rolled up your sleeves to wash your hands."

"And why the long sleeves? The weather's been warm lately. We've all been wearing shorts, and you still dress like it's winter," Miranda said.

I knew what she was doing—the good cop, bad cop thing—but I didn't think that was going to work on Deb.

"What's with the attitude, Miranda?" Deb was getting riled up. "Are you jealous? I'm losing weight and you're not?"

"Of course not," Miranda spat out. "Bottom line, you're too damn skinny, Deb. Whatever you're doing needs to stop."

Everything began to spin out of control.

"Don't get on your high horse and tell me what I can and can't do, Miranda Donahue."

The rhyme struck me funny and I snorted. They both looked at me. "The rhyme can't do, Miranda Donahue." I shrugged when they failed to see the humor.

"Are you binging and purging?" Miranda asked pointedly.

"Fuck you! Did Angel tell you that?" Deb jumped to her feet.

I jumped, too. "Now wait, Angel didn't say anything." I looked back at Miranda with daggers in my eyes. "Miranda just asked a question. It's reasonable from where we're standing."

"Where you're standing is outside. Get the hell out of my house!"

"Deb, please," I said, hoping for just a tendril of reasoning. The door slamming on my ass dismissed all chances of that.

"What happened in there?" I asked Miranda angrily when we got into my car.

"We weren't getting anywhere. I was trying to fluster her so she would slip up and admit what she was doing."

I rubbed my pounding forehead. "I cannot believe you asked her straight up if she binged and purged."

"Well, how else were we gonna do it?" Miranda said angrily. "With Deb, you just have to jump in there sometimes. Maybe now that she knows we suspect what she's doing, she'll stop."

"I think we both know it's not that simple. Let her cool down for a while and maybe we can reason with her."

Miranda scrubbed at her face. "I guess the cookout on the beach is off."

I almost reached over and patted her arm and stopped mid-reach. "Let it ride for a while."

Miranda huffed, then sighed loudly. "Let's go to the gym. I have some anxiety to work off. You think you can handle being around Jade?"

I nodded. "She's all business when she's at work. I think I can keep to my side of the gym."

When we arrived, I almost went outside to see if it was a full moon because everyone seemed to be pissed off. Miranda was tortured by the encounter with Deb, and Jade wasn't much better. We passed her in the hall as we were going to the locker room to change. "Hey, Jade," I said cheerfully.

Her eyes were cold when she looked at us. "Hey," she said and kept on walking.

"Got a bug in her ass tonight, too." Miranda looked over her shoulder and watched as Jade stomped into the gym.

I tried to focus on stretching out, but I couldn't help but glance in the mirror at Jade as she talked to whom I presumed was a newbie to the gym.

Unlike Miranda and me, who looked like we bought our workout gear secondhand, this woman was in what appeared to be new duds. The Nike swoosh was on everything from her shoes to her socks. Her matching shirt and shorts also sported the logo. Her face was made up, too, including what I liked to call hooker red lipstick. Most people took off their jewelry when exercising but not this woman. She was sporting more bling than most actors did on the red carpet.

Wealth and privilege oozed from her pores, and I wondered why she wasn't in one of the upscale gyms in Tallahassee instead of this backwater hole in the woods.

I felt immediate dislike shoot through me as she moved close to Jade every time she spoke. Jade would take a step back, and the woman would step closer. When Jade began demonstrating how to use the equipment, the woman watched with a slight smile on her face. I didn't have to touch her to know that she wasn't truly interested in what the machines could do for her, but rather Jade's body as it flexed and moved. When it came her turn to try, she didn't appear to give much effort. The displeasure on Jade's face was reminiscent of the way she looked at me when she thought I was a player.

"Come on, time for the damn lunges." Miranda got into position and stared up at me until I fell in step.

I caught Jade watching us. The newbie next to her followed her gaze and our eyes met. My dislike of her rose as I noticed the dismissal. She looked at me and Miranda like we were a distraction she shouldn't have to tolerate. She put her hand on Jade's arm, forcing her to look away.

I was jealous. Not just because this woman had her attention, but she could do something I'd always taken for granted. She could touch without having to worry about being slammed into someone else's consciousness. She could enjoy the simplicity of touch, the warmth and softness of another's skin. It made me burn.

"This isn't doing you any good."

I looked back at Miranda. She was standing with her hands on her hips, her expression sad.

"You can't even focus, you're so drawn to her. Maybe we should buy some equipment and work out at home."

"You said I shouldn't lock myself away anymore. I should get back into my routines." I immediately felt discouraged because I knew what she meant. I had to back away from Jade. I had to go on with my life like it had been before Jade came to Panacea.

Miranda narrowed her eyes. "You know what I mean."

As much as I tried to ignore Jade, I couldn't. I'd get into what I was doing and she'd walk by or I'd hear her voice, and I'd be distracted again. We left before we'd done half of the program.

Miranda was sitting at my kitchen table stroking the bridge of her nose. I didn't say anything because I knew she was deep in thought, trying to work the puzzle that had become my life. I sat next to her and propped my chin in my hand and waited for her to acknowledge me.

"When you come in contact with someone, the video immediately starts to play, and you feel what they feel, right?"

"Like I'm in their body, yes."

"Okay, how about you touch me, but focus on what you're feeling? Try to feel my skin, focus on that." She put her hand out, and I stared at it for a second before I reached over and laid mine upon hers.

Miranda was sleepy. The words on the page had begun to blur a bit. She looked over at Marty, who was lying in the bathtub. Her eyes were closed, but her brow had a stark line through it as she concentrated on what Miranda was reading.

The connection broke when Miranda pulled her hand away.

"Do you realize you just made me see your wife naked?"

Miranda's face turned red as she frowned. "You weren't supposed to see that."

"You read to her in the bathtub, that's so sweet."

"Marty's learning a new computer system at work. She falls asleep anytime she reads the manual, so I try to help." Miranda thrust out her hand again. "Feel my skin, the calluses on my hand. Focus on *that*."

Miranda's hand lay palm up. I looked at her skin, the tiny lines, the pale calluses and tried to imagine what they'd feel like under my fingertips. With that in mind, I touched her lightly. Images tried to come, but I mentally shoved them back. In my mind's eye, I could see the image blurry like it was a video on pause. I stared hard at Miranda's palm, focusing solely on what it felt like. Miranda's feelings bubbled up in me like a spring. Those I could not stop. She was curious, hopeful, and somewhere far back worried about Deb.

This time, I broke the connection and grinned. "I stopped it. I didn't go into your mind. I could still feel your emotions, though."

Miranda jumped in her seat. "Could you feel my skin?"

"Yes," I said, matching her enthusiasm. "It was like I was forcing two sides of my brain to work in unison. I saw your hand, I felt it."

Miranda stroked the bridge of her nose twice as she looked at me. "You hated math and daydreamed in class all the time. Do you remember admitting that to me?"

"Yeah, and I remember Mom going ballistic when I got a D my first semester in high school."

"Right. Then you forced yourself to pay attention. You had to train your brain to listen and focus. I think you're gonna have to do the same with this." She pounded her hands on the table. "You can do this. You just have to practice."

I clapped my hands together and stared at the ceiling. I was seeing light at the end of a dark tunnel I thought I'd never crawl out of.

"Look at me," Miranda said, drawing my attention. "You can harness this crazy thing. You can have it all, you just have to work really hard. Think of it as a tool you can use when you need to but put in a box when you don't."

I liked that analogy.

"We'll practice together as much as you need." She grinned. "I'm with you most of the time, anyway. I'm happy to be your guinea pig."

I looked at her, and the love in my heart overwhelmed me. She was more dedicated to me than my own brother whom I rarely saw on holidays and occasionally sent an e-mail or postcard. "I wish I could hug you."

Miranda looked surprised and pleased at my admission. "Do it. Try to focus on what you feel, but if you slip into my mind, I don't care. I trust you, and there's nothing I keep from you."

We stood and looked at each other awkwardly for a minute. We'd slept in the same bed, one showered while the other used the toilet, but when it came to showing affection, we stumbled. It was my fault, I knew that. Miranda had always been so open, but I was the one who held back. She understood it and never pushed, knowing that I loved her just the same.

I took the step and watched as her arms opened. I felt them enclose me tightly and the press of her body to mine. Images came, and I pushed against them hard in my mind. She whispered, "I love you," over and over, and I felt it, nothing but love in its purest, most innocent form.

I lost myself in her embrace, and for a second, I forgot to fight. Images came before I could stop them. I knew it was the day we stopped being friends and became sisters. I felt the sun on my face—Miranda's face—the roughness of the rope in my hands. I was balancing on a limb, my bare feet clutched to it like a bird. I felt the muscles in my stomach and arms tighten as I pushed off. The weightlessness was exciting and scary as I swung out high and free. Then I felt my grip slipping, the horror of letting go, and the pain when I crashed to the ground. My ankle was filled with waves of agony that would subside and come back stronger with each beat of my heart.

I looked up through her eyes at myself. Concern and fear etched my childish face as I fought through the brambles.

"I think I broke my foot," Miranda was saying it, but I felt the effort it took to utter the words, the sob rising deep out of my chest.

I watched the vision of myself kneel down and felt the touch of my own hand on Miranda's knee. "It's okay, I'll carry you," I heard myself say. "Everything's gonna be okay, don't cry." The compassion in my voice was evident.

"I'm too heavy, go get Momma," I felt Miranda say.

I watched myself shake my head. "I'm not leaving you out here alone." My face was contorted in fear. "I won't leave you."

I felt the realization in Miranda's mind. *She loves me, she won't let me down.* The tender bond that formed and carried us through adulthood blossomed right there on that hot summer day.

Miranda stepped back and broke the connection. She waggled a finger at me. "You got in my brain. Practice, practice, prac—" She stopped when she saw the look on my face. "What, what did you see? Was it sad again?"

I shook my head, unable to speak.

Miranda grimaced. "You look upset. I want to hug you again, but I don't think I should."

"It wasn't bad." My voice came out in a croak. "I saw…the day…the time you realized that I loved you and you loved me. The day we became sisters."

I watched the wheels turn behind Miranda's eyes. "What day was that exactly?" She held her hands up when I looked disappointed. "Sloan, there were so many."

"The day we made the rope swing and you broke your ankle."

"You were my hero that day." Miranda smiled wistfully.

"Well…" I stuffed my hands in my pockets. "You're my hero today."

Chapter 9

I usually skipped the health club on the days Miranda worked her shift, but…I wanted to see Jade. I knew Miranda was right. I needed to avoid her until I got my brain under control. I reasoned that at the health club we wouldn't have any time alone, and I could just observe Jade from afar. I had no reference for what it felt like to fall in love, but I thought I barely knew Jade, and what Miranda claimed was the beginning of love was just curiosity out of control.

I even waved off the tiny jump my heart made when I spotted her as I came in the door. She was wearing a pair of black shorts with reflective piping that went around the edges. A black sleeveless T-shirt clung tightly to her body. Her back was to me when I started my stretches, and I was content to occasionally glance her way. Just being in the same room with her made me feel something I didn't recognize.

I looked into the mirror and caught her eye as she watched me. It felt like something passed between us. She smiled, a real smile that transformed her face, not the work smile. I found myself grinning until *she* walked into the room.

Miss Bling was wearing a light blue shirt that matched her shorts. The band around the top of her ankle socks matched the whole ensemble. She walked right up and put a hand on Jade's arm, and whatever was flowing between us came to a screeching halt.

I started hefting weights like a body builder. I was grunting and puffing with the men alongside me, although their weights were significantly heavier. I despised the newcomer and needed to dispel the angry energy that flowed through me whenever I looked at her. I'd never truly known jealousy; the feeling was foreign, and I hated it. I also despised the fact that the flirtatious woman could make me feel it, like she had some power over me I couldn't control.

My gaze wandered and I found Jade again. She had the bitch in blue doing lunges. I watched her make one pass across the gym and begin to protest. Jade seemed to be arguing with her. I watched the tiny muscle flicker in her cheek as Jade clamped her jaw tightly. The woman was smiling and saying something that had no effect on Jade's ire. That made me smile.

I'd noticed that Jade usually spent an hour with each client. Usually after she was finished with them, they looked like they'd been through a fierce battle, red-faced and breathing heavily. This woman did not. Instead of gulping down water and limping toward the door as the others did, she hung around watching as Jade worked with another one of her victims.

This was a turning point for me. I had been avoiding touch, but I wanted to touch this woman. I was fairly certain what she had on her mind, but I wouldn't be satisfied until I had her number completely. I contemplated offering my hand for her to shake but thought better of it because that would poke holes in my germaphobe lie. The latter idea was more plausible. I would trip and fall on her. I did just that as I strolled toward the locker room. The collision was a sound one. I acted as though I tripped on my own feet and launched my body into hers.

Her feelings were the first thing that assaulted me—lust, desire, the need to possess. I let the images come with no resistance. She was sitting idly at a table on a sun porch. I felt the coolness of the spoon that she toyed with and finally laid next to a cup of tea. Her gaze settled on an older man who looked familiar as he read *The Washington Post*. "I'm working with a personal trainer. She has an amazing body."

The man turned down one corner of the paper and smiled. She was pleased, then I realized this was a game between them. It was like digging through a file cabinet in her mind, I went through everything I could find. She wasn't a lesbian, not even bisexual really. But it turned her on incredibly that he was aroused by her exploits. She'd brought many a woman to their bed while he watched unbeknownst to the new lover.

"She's playing hard to get, but I'll bend her to my will." The paper didn't move, and she continued. "You're gonna like seeing me in her arms. Watch her sexy mouth move across my body." The paper did move then, and I realized I knew this man from somewhere. I dug deeper into her mind until I found his name. Robert Priest was a high-powered lawyer who had recently been elected as senator in Florida. She was his toy, and he kept her tucked away in a beach house in the obscure area of Alligator Point.

No one knew Jacquelyn Marlow, but that would change, she thought. She'd played the game well for a few years and earned his trust. And soon she'd let word and pictures of their affair leak to the press, and everyone and his brother would want her story as mistress to the man who had his eye on the presidency. That it would ruin his career was of no consequence to her. He was a liar and a cheat, and it would feel good to step on his neck to elevate herself to fame. Jade was only a toy in the back of her mind.

She pushed at me roughly and broke the connection. "What's wrong with you?" she asked angrily.

"I tripped." I stayed on my hands and knees. "It knocked the breath out of me."

Not one ounce of compassion showed in her eyes, rather a disgust for coming in physical contact with the likes of me.

Strong hands gripped my arms, and I felt myself rise up like a feather-light rag doll. I didn't have to look to know it was Jade. I fought to keep a mental hold on the feel of her hands and marvel at her strength, but my newly acquired skill was no match for the strong feelings and images her touch evoked.

"My client list is booked," Jade argued. "I'm actually carrying more than the usual."

"She's paying double to be trained by you," her boss said. "Doesn't it stroke your ego to know that someone wants to work with you that badly?"

"We both know it's not because she wants to get in shape. She doesn't do half of what I tell her. Whatever her reasons are it's not because of my reputation as a trainer," Jade said hotly.

"She's yours, accommodate her."

Jade released me when I was firmly on my feet. My gaze was locked with Jacquelyn's. "Are you okay?" Jade asked, making me look at her. I glanced back at Jacquelyn, and I could see the fury on her face at being the one ignored.

"I'm fine, thanks." I walked away without another word. I left the gym without going to the locker room to get my bag. Rage surged through me, and I was afraid of it. The hostility I felt for Jacquelyn shocked me. I'd never laid a hand on anyone in anger, but in her case, I was more than willing to make an exception.

In the shower, I scrubbed my body roughly to get whatever germs had been deposited on me from being in contact with someone as despicable as Jacquelyn. I was even more pissed that I had scrubbed with equal fervor the places on my arms where Jade had touched me. I wanted that touch to remain on my skin.

I was too mad to eat and too mad to sleep. I plopped down on the couch and stared at the TV, trying to purge all that I'd seen from my mind and wondering what I'd do with the knowledge. I'd been sitting there for an hour when I heard a soft knock on my door. I knew it wasn't Miranda; she'd just let herself in. So I peeked through the window and was surprised to see Jade looking nervous as she stood on the porch with my gym bag in her hands. I opened the door and looked at her.

"Uh…hey." She held up the bag. "You left this. I could've just stored it for you until you came back…but I wanted to see if you were okay."

"How'd you find me?" I stepped back and let her in.

"Your wallet was inside, that's the other reason I brought it. I thought you might need it."

"Thanks. You want some water or juice?" I said as I moved deeper into the room, drawing her in.

"Water would be great, thanks."

She followed me into the kitchen. I watched her as I reached into the fridge for a bottle. She was looking around the room curiously. "Thanks," she said with a nod when I handed her the water.

"You wanna sit down?"

Her gaze darted to the clock, and she frowned. "It's kind of late. Are you sure I'm not keeping you up?"

"I'm not going to be able to sleep for a while." She looked at me funny, and I figured it was the aggravation in my tone.

She followed me back into the living room where I sat in a chair and pulled my legs up beneath me. She took a spot on the couch and opened her water. I watched her drink half of it before she replaced the lid.

"Thanks for helping me up after my accident."

Jade shrugged. "You weren't moving. I was afraid that you'd really gotten hurt."

"She's a real bitch." The words popped out of my mouth quickly, and I found that I felt no guilt.

Jade's expression was unrecognizable. I wasn't sure if she was angry or sad. "I'm used to her kind. She fits into one of two categories. One are those who come for the fitness, the other comes to pick up a body. She, of course, is in the latter." Jade shrugged again. "If you want to have a fling with a fit body, the health club is the perfect pickup point." She grinned at me. "But you know all about that."

I hated that at one time Jade had lumped me into the same category as Jacquelyn, and I didn't return her smile. I knew the answer to my next question, but I wanted to hear what Jade had to say anyway. "Why'd you accept her as a client?"

"I had no choice." Her tone was bitter. "She paid extra to have me as a trainer because I was booked and my boss agreed to it." She squeezed the bottle in her hand. "I worked hard to schedule my clients during the week so I could have my weekends off." Jade gestured wildly as she spoke. "I work twelve-hour days as it is, and unless I can talk one of my clients into another trainer, I'll have to come in half a day on Saturdays."

Again, I knew what Jade's answer would be, but I wanted to see the expression on her face. "Then why does she have to have you as a trainer if she just wants to screw off?"

Jade looked embarrassed. "She asks me out every time she comes to the gym. I don't think she's rejected often, and I think she sees it as a challenge."

"Can't you tell her that what she's doing is harassment?"

Jade took a swallow from her bottle. "Not if I want to keep my job. Money talks in this world, Sloan. I'm sure you know that."

"Okay, what if you resigned and took your clients with you?"

"Where would we work out? I can't afford to buy a gym of my own." She looked as if the idea had crossed her mind many times.

"Ever think about doing something else?"

My heart sank as her shoulders slumped. "I don't know anything else."

"You could go back to school, learn a new trade."

Jade shot me that fake smile. "Did you miss the part where I said I work twelve-hour days? I can't afford to lose the income. I have bills to pay."

I chewed the inside of my cheek. "Want to hear a funny story? Maybe take your mind off things?"

She nodded, and a tiny real smile graced her face.

"Miranda and I have a friend who we believe may have an eating disorder. We confronted her about it, and she threw us out of her house."

"That's…not really funny," Jade said with a grimace.

"No, I guess not. It's all I got, though."

"You have a nice place." She looked around the room, and her gaze settled on the picture of Miranda and me on vacation. I'd framed it and set it on the shelf above my TV.

"That was taken right before I went through the ice."

Jade looked back at me. "You really do sound casual when you talk about it."

"I guess since I don't remember the horror of going through the ice that it doesn't affect me. It's the after-effects I have to deal with now." I bit my lip knowing I shouldn't have admitted that last bit.

"Will you tell me about it one day?"

I couldn't meet her gaze. "Maybe, then again if you knew, you might wish you didn't."

"What could be so bad about it?" I could hear the honest curiosity in her voice.

"Have you ever read about near-death experiences, or NDEs, as they're known? There's a lot of stuff about them on the Internet."

She shook her head. "I don't have a computer at home, and surfing at work is discouraged."

I supposed that I asked the question to gauge her reaction. I figured that maybe after the first time I'd admitted it that maybe she had done some research on her own. I wanted to know if she accepted some of the claims of others like being more sensitive to light and sound and a heightened awareness, though nobody seemed to be like me. "I feel weird, and on some days, like a circus act."

She smiled then. "I have those days, too."

"I'm sure you do," I said with a nod.

"I have to go." Jade stood abruptly. "Guy will be hungry."

I wanted to touch her so bad. Just a little pat to let her know I cared. I focused on her arm, what it would feel like under my hand. She was walking ahead of me to the door. I reached out and touched her shoulder. I felt the warmth beneath my palm, the fabric of her shirt and pulled away quickly when my mind began to soar. She turned and looked at me surprised. "Tell Guy I said hello."

"I will," she said with a smile.

I watched her go down the walk as the tiny thread of feeling I got from her settled deep in the pit of my stomach. She liked me—a lot.

Chapter 10

I watched Miranda walk into the store. Instead of doughnuts and chocolate milk, she put two containers of yogurt and juice on the counter. It came out in a rush. I had to admit what I'd done. "I went to the health club last night, I saw Jade, I touched that new client of hers, she's unbelievably evil, I left my bag, Jade came to the house with it, we talked."

Miranda stood, blinking under the assault. Once it had fermented in her brain, she slapped her forehead. "My God, you are completely out of control!"

"I know, I know," I cried as I danced around in a circle, hoping she would laugh and forget to be pissed. She didn't. I stopped dancing and tried to look contrite.

Miranda came around the counter, popped the top on her yogurt, and pointed her spoon at me. "Tell me everything you did from the minute you left this store. Share the details of your touchings if you think you should."

In glorious graphic detail, I told her everything. At times, she would cough when she got choked on her yogurt or juice. When I finished, she sat rubbing the bridge of her nose. "I can't believe you're sitting right on top of a scandal."

I hadn't given much thought to Senator Priest and Jacquelyn Marlow. They were rotten in my opinion, and whatever they did to each other...well, that was their problem. I just didn't want Jade to become a part of it. Miranda was blown away by the revelation and appeared to be focused on that, so I felt I was in the clear with Jade. Not so.

"I told you that she was going to like you." Miranda waved

her spoon again. "Now what're you going to do with that?"

"I was thinking that maybe...I could tell her the truth."

Miranda stared at me. The plastic yogurt spoon she had been tapping her leg with clattered to the floor. She began rubbing the bridge of her nose furiously. "You trust her that much?"

"I want to."

Miranda's voice was low and calm. "But do you know in your heart that Jade won't tell everyone what you're able to do?"

In my heart, I knew she would keep my secret. I nodded slowly.

Miranda sighed. "Now here's the hard part. How do you think she'll react to the knowledge that you've been in her mind and have been privy to her innermost thoughts and memories?"

I put myself in Jade's shoes, and I would've been livid. I probably wouldn't have trusted her no matter how much she explained. "Shit."

"Shit is right." Miranda looked so sorry for me. "It's your choice who you want to tell. I just want you to be prepared for what you're probably going to face."

I put my hands on my hips. "I'm screwed either way. If I don't tell her, I won't be able to get close to her. If I do tell her, I probably won't be able to get close to her."

"There's something else for you to consider." Miranda looked miserable as she said, "You could walk away and meet someone else that maybe you could be honest with at the very beginning."

"I don't want to walk away. Of all people, I think she'd understand the most once she...forgave me."

"Could she? Do you know that about her?"

I couldn't readily answer that question. To make matters worse, my cell phone rang, and when I answered, it was Jade.

"Hey, Sloan, I have a huge favor to ask, and if you can't do it, don't worry. I'll come up with something else."

I looked at Miranda, who was staring at me. "What's up?"

"I took Guy in to be neutered today, and they want him picked up by six. I'm not going to be able to get out of here like I'd hoped." She hesitated for a minute. "Could you possibly pick him up for me?"

The answer was going to be yes regardless of what Miranda and I discussed. "Of course."

"I've already paid for everything. All you have to do is pick him up."

"He's probably not going to be comfortable at the gym. Do you want me to pick up the keys to your apartment and take him there?"

The line went silent for a few seconds. "Um…no. Would it be a problem if I picked him up at your place?"

I didn't ask why. For some reason, I knew I shouldn't. "Okay, I'll bring him home and you can come by whenever you're ready."

The relief in her voice was palpable. "Thanks. I can't tell you how much I appreciate this. I'll see you tonight."

I snapped the phone shut and looked sheepishly at Miranda. Her shoulders slumped as she sighed.

I opened the kennel when I got home and gave Guy the option of coming out if he wanted to. He didn't seem interested. I put down a bowl of water and a bowl of the sample kitty food they gave me at the vet's office. The receptionist was even kind enough to give me a cardboard box with some litter in it in case Guy had to potty before Jade arrived. Apparently, she didn't realize I was also the bringer of Sparky, or she probably wouldn't have been as helpful.

I made myself some dinner and ate in front of the TV. I even made Jade a plate and kept it warm in case she was hungry. If not, it'd be my lunch for the next day. She arrived a little after nine.

Guy came out of the kennel then, and I sat back with a smile as they enjoyed their reunion. Jade sat Indian style on the floor, and Guy crawled all over her lap bumping his face against hers. She laughed like a child and reveled in his feline affection.

"Thank you so much, Sloan. My stomach was in knots when I realized I wasn't going to be able to leave work. I hated the thought of him spending the night up there wondering why I had abandoned him."

"I was happy to do it, and I'm happy you asked. Are you hungry?"

Jade looked up and smiled. "I'm always hungry."

"Well, you're in luck because I cooked up one of those low-fat casseroles that was in the handout you gave me." I stood and stretched. "What would you like to drink? Milk, water, or juice?"

"Milk would be great. Can I help with anything?"

"Nope. Enjoy your cat while I get it together."

I spooned a healthy pile onto Jade's plate, then I poured her a tall glass of milk. It felt good to do this for her. Aside from Momma Donahue and Miranda, I'd never really cooked for anyone. It made me feel domesticated, a strange feeling I decided I liked.

"Are you going to eat, too?" Jade asked as she walked into the kitchen.

"No, I've already eaten, but I'll keep you company." I set her plate and glass on the table and poured myself a glass of juice. Jade was waiting, her food untouched, until I sat down. Then she went at it like a woman who hadn't eaten in days.

"I should be the one feeding you for what you've done." She wiped her mouth with a napkin. "Do you like Chinese?"

"Love it." That was kind of a lie. I only marginally liked Chinese food because I couldn't figure out what the hell most of it was.

"Would you like to have dinner with me Saturday night?"

I couldn't help the smile that spread across my face. "Yes."

She blushed a little and went back to her meal. After she finished, she insisted on washing her dishes and my juice glass. We argued playfully as she dried them and replaced everything in the cabinet. I wanted the evening to last and was disappointed when she said, "I better go. We both have to get up early in the morning."

I watched as she tucked Guy in the kennel and set it by the door. She stood up straight and smiled. My touch the other night must've changed something in the dynamic of our friendship. She took it as permission to bypass my germaphobe barrier, and she hugged me tightly.

Images of women flashed through my mind. Associated with

each face that passed was the overwhelming feeling of being used by each one. I felt her resignation that the dalliances she experienced were the only affection she was worthy to receive. And then I saw myself and felt her excitement, her hope that I might be different. When she released me, I staggered back and fell onto the couch. She looked at me in shock and reached out to touch me.

"Don't," I nearly shouted and climbed over the back of the couch to avoid her. The devastation on her face tore my heart in two.

"I'm sorry," she said, sounding hurt and confused. She turned abruptly, yanked the door open, and bent to pick up the kennel.

"Jade, wait!" I moved toward her and stopped short. "Please let me explain."

I watched as she straightened slowly, her face flushed and pained. "What's so wrong with me?"

"Nothing, absolutely nothing. But there's something wrong with me, and I need to tell you about it. Please sit down and hear me out for a minute." She closed the door and turned slowly. I backed up to my chair and sat. "Please sit...I think you're going to need to."

She sat on the edge of the couch and planted her hands on either side of her like she was poised to slide into a pool, but the water was too cold. "Sloan, are you...ill? Do you have something termina—"

"I'm not sick." I watched as she sagged slightly in relief. She wouldn't look at me, and I was biting my knuckle until I realized how bad it hurt. "I don't know how to explain this, how much you'll believe, but I swear I'm not going to lie to you."

She nodded and waited.

"You know I've been struggling with a change since my accident, you've asked me about it."

She nodded again, and I noticed that she slid back a couple of inches on the couch. She was preparing herself for the long story.

"When I touch someone...I see things." Her gaze darted to mine and away quickly. "I feel things, too. I see...their memories as if I were living them myself, and I feel their emotions." I sat silent, waiting for her reaction.

"Like the Stephen King book where the guy saw the future when he touched people?" Her voice sounded odd and distant.

"Sort of, but I see memories and feel emotion. I can't see a person's future."

She looked majorly disappointed. "You promised you wouldn't lie to me," she said accusingly. "Did I misjudge you? Are you straight?"

"No," I said confused. "No, I'm not."

"Then why does it gross you out so bad to touch me?" She stood. "Wait, don't tell me. I don't want to know." There was no anger in her voice, just resignation.

"I saw the night that your boss tried to force you to have drinks...or whatever with him. I felt the mud sucking at your shoes. The angry tears you wiped away when you had to walk home."

Jade froze. Her eyes were huge, and even though what I said shocked her, I could tell she was trying to figure out how I knew.

"I saw...felt you talking to Lauren. How you felt when you decided you wouldn't call her anymore. You knew she was having an affair with you, and you believed the lie as long as you could. Just now when you hugged me, I saw the faces of all the women you thought of and how you felt used, and you...hoped I might be different. I am—"

"Stop!" she yelled. She took a deep breath and held up her hand. "Just stop for a minute."

I couldn't. "Jade, that's why I didn't touch you. Why I avoided you touching me. I felt like I was invading your privacy."

"I asked you to stop." Her voice trembled. She sat slowly on the edge of the couch again. She didn't appear to want to, but her legs seemed to give out. "When the guy dropped a weight on my foot...you touched me." Her fingers were tapping her leg like she was counting in her head. My heart felt like it stalled in my chest. "All this time...you knew."

"I'm sorry. I—"

"For what?" she said angrily. "For seeing how pathetic I really am?" Tears streamed out of her eyes.

I got out of my chair and walked toward her, wanting to take her into my arms so bad it physically hurt. When she realized what I intended, her eyes went round and she jumped up. "Were you going to touch me again? Haven't you seen enough?" Her voice broke. "Why were you even going to go out with me?"

I stood stock-still with my arms limply at my side. "I really like you. I want to get to know you."

Jade shook her head like she was trying to wake from a bad dream. "How could you?" She sounded so wounded.

"I won't use you like the others. I—" She gasped as the gravity of it all seemed to hit her. She backed away, tripped over the kennel, and fell into the doorjamb. I moved toward her.

"Stop!" She held her hands up after she righted herself. "Don't touch me again." She grabbed the kennel. "I don't want to see you again. If you come to the gym, I'll quit."

I watched her run down the walk with Guy in his kennel, climb into her truck, and speed away. In a matter of minutes, I'd crushed her hope, and she'd crushed mine.

Chapter 11

I didn't open the store next day. I knew people would see the "closed" sign and maybe come back later. I didn't care. I slept on and off, never more than an hour. I lay in bed in that dream-like state from exhaustion. I was hurting in ways I never imagined, and I knew Jade was, too. If Miranda was right and what I felt was the precursor to love, I wondered why anyone would seek such a thing.

I had just drifted into merciful sleep when I heard the bedroom door open. Wordlessly, Miranda crawled into bed next to me, carefully keeping her distance. "You told her," she said softly.

"She hates me." My voice sounded dull, lacking emotion. "She told me she never wants to see me again. She'll quit the gym if I go back there."

"I'm so sorry, Sloan."

"I don't want to hear any 'pick yourself up by your bootstraps' speeches right now."

"I wouldn't do that," Miranda said in the darkness. I could just make out her silhouette. "You need your time to grieve."

"Why do you trust Marty?"

Miranda was silent for a minute or two. "I couldn't help it."

The concept seemed foreign to me then. I was more willing to trust someone to pull me from a burning building or a cliff's edge but never with my feelings. I had no idea how Miranda could trust Marty with her vulnerabilities, reveal her innermost secrets, and trust that they'd be accepted and cherished. Miranda had been the only one I trusted, but it wasn't the same way I wanted to trust in Jade.

"I know she's out there hurting, and I'm the cause. I don't know her phone number. Every time she called, it was from the gym, and I have no idea where she lives. I can't even go to her and beg her to forgive me." I swallowed the lump in my throat. "She's a runner. She admitted to living a lot of places. Every time she gets hurt, she pulls up stakes and starts somewhere else. What if she runs, Miranda? I know I'll never see her again."

Miranda didn't say anything. I knew she couldn't. If she were to be honest, she'd have to say, "Let her go." I couldn't.

"I wish I could hold you," Miranda said. She was close enough for me to feel her breath on my face.

"I wish you could, too. I'm too weak to fight my brain, and we both know what will happen."

"So what? Get lost in my memories for a while. Maybe it'll put you to sleep. You already know all my stories." I rolled onto her shoulder, and as her arms went around me, I began to live vicariously through Miranda. I felt her deep sorrow for me as I watched her memories unfold before my eyes.

A week went by, and I tearfully begged Miranda to go work out at the gym to make sure Jade was still there. She stayed gone for an hour and returned to me. "She's still there." I stared at her, awaiting anything she could tell me. "She looks bad. Dark circles are under her eyes. I don't know if it makes you feel any better to know she looks just like you."

"Did she talk to you?"

"No." Miranda looked away. "When she first saw me come in, I think she was looking for you. She stopped staring, I guess, when she figured out it was just me."

"Should I take that as a good sign? Maybe she wanted to see me?"

Miranda plopped down on the couch and propped her feet on the table. "I don't know. She might've wanted to see you, or she might've been ready to bolt if she did."

I opened my mouth to say something but sighed instead.

"Are you about to ask me if I would talk to her?"

"Yes," I said, exasperated.

"I thought about it tonight, but there was no way I could do it privately."

"She usually leaves work around nine. Drives a blue beat-up Ford truck."

Miranda groaned and looked at her watch. "If you have a cookie or something sweet, I'll do it." Six Oreos later, Miranda walked out the door pissed that I had them and had kept them hidden. I waited and paced. Thirty minutes passed, and she still wasn't back. I took that as a good sign. An hour passed, even better, but the waiting was driving me insane. I saw headlights on the street and ripped the door open only to watch an unfamiliar car pass. I paced some more. Two hours had passed since Miranda had left, and I debated sending a text message. I put it off for thirty more minutes, then I heard a car door slam.

I was standing in the doorway when Miranda came up the steps. "Did you talk to her?"

I stepped back inside when I noticed that Miranda's eyes were red and tear-stained. "Sit down, Sloan," she said somberly.

"I don't think I can."

"Please." Miranda pointed to the couch, and reluctantly, I sat. She sank down on the other end. "That girl cried her eyes out on my shoulder. She's as pitiful as you are."

I swallowed hard and ached inside.

"She admitted that she really likes you. She hoped to get to know you and thought something good might develop."

I smiled and felt so much relief that I thought I would cry again if I could, then it struck me that Miranda was talking in the past tense.

"I had to swear on my mother's grave that you did not tell me anything of what you saw about her before she would talk to me. I think that ratcheted her trust up a little bit." Miranda rubbed her hands on her gym pants. "Right now, she's grappling with the shock of what you told her. We talked a lot about that. I think it made her feel a bit better to know how much of a struggle this has been for you. That it wasn't something you took lightly."

"You told her I felt bad about prying?"

"Many times." Miranda looked over at me. "She feels terribly exposed. You saw things that she'd never admitted to anyone. She didn't go into detail, but I gathered that her past has been extremely painful."

Jade's memories flashed through my mind on fast forward. "Yeah, she's had a rough time of it."

"She…needs some time." Miranda smiled weakly. "I don't want to get your hopes up. She said we'll talk again soon."

"Meaning you and her, not me."

Miranda reached for me and stopped. "Yeah. But that's a start. She isn't running, so that tells me that eventually she might be willing to give you a chance, which is why it's so important for us to continue your mental workouts."

I took it for it what it was—a chance and a glimmer of hope. "Okay then, go home and get some rest. We'll hit it hard tomorrow."

Chapter 12

Of course, Jade and I did not go on our planned date. Miranda and I spent weeks working on my brain. I had good days and bad. The bad ones came when I was tired and couldn't focus. I was on a roller coaster of highs and lows. The day Miranda came into the store with good news, I was particularly low, but what she said sent me soaring.

"Jade says you can come back to work out at the gym if you want."

I was so excited, I could barely speak.

"Easy, Sparky Junior, that doesn't mean you're gonna pick up where you left off. She basically meant she wouldn't leave if you showed up. She's still not ready to talk to you yet."

It was a start and more than I had hoped for. "I'll leave her alone. She can approach me if she wants to…when she's ready."

"Good," Miranda said with a nod. "Marty talked to Deb. She gave her a while to cool down."

I raised a brow.

"She's still furious with us. Marty reminded her of how much we love her, and she said Deb sort of chilled after that." Miranda smiled. "Marty's so good at that kind of thing. I guess we should've sent her in first. She didn't ask Deb about the weight thing. She just let her bitch, but she thinks she might get Deb to gradually open up to her. So we're gonna delay Lonna and Paige's surprise party until things are smoothed over."

Lonna and Paige returned from Provincetown as a married couple. I pretended to be just as shocked as everyone else by the news. Marty wanted to have a reception-slash-party for them, but with the tension among Miranda, Deb, and me, we'd put it off for a while. Unlike Jade, Deb wasn't willing to be in the same room with us.

"She'll come around," I said.

Miranda nodded as she ran her index finger down the bridge of her nose. She'd been the most vocal and intrusive in our conversation with Deb, and I figured she felt she alone shouldered the fault that Deb had placed on us. "So we'll go to the gym tonight at six?"

"Yeah, and I promise to behave myself." I held up a hand like I was taking an oath.

"Okay, I'll meet you there. Don't go in without me."

"Where are you going?" I asked, surprised that she wasn't going to stay with me.

Miranda smiled. "I've got a lunch date with Marty. Haven't seen her much lately." She pointed at me when my shoulders slumped guiltily. "Stop feeling bad. She understands you need me."

"What've you been telling her?"

"You're still coping with the accident. That's not a lie, you know."

That Miranda had to clarify that statement told me that she felt maybe she wasn't being totally honest with Marty. "I think I...we should tell her the truth. I'm close to her, too, and I think she should know. We could accidentally touch."

I could tell by the way Miranda's body seemed to relax that she'd been waiting to hear that. The burden of keeping my secret, especially from her partner, was a lot to carry. "That's your decision."

"Maybe I could go home with you after the gym tonight?"

"Sure." Miranda's grin was huge. "I gotta run. I'll see you at six."

I sat in the parking lot staring at Jade's truck, feeling completely nervous. I wasn't sure how seeing her again was going to make me feel. I prepared myself for the chance that she might ignore me altogether. And then there was Marty. My suggestion to tell her had been bouncing around for a while. It wasn't a spur-of-the-moment thing when I suggested it to Miranda. Once it was out of my mouth, I committed myself to doing it because I was afraid that if I mulled it over any longer, I'd lose my nerve.

Miranda's car pulled up alongside mine, and I released a long breath before I got out. "You okay?" she asked the minute she opened her door.

"Nope, but I'm ready as I'll ever be."

We walked into the gym and dropped our bags off in the locker room. As we walked down the hall, I had a feeling I was about to walk out on stage when we entered the gym. My performance would have to be a good one. I knew I couldn't hide behind a mask of stoicism. I'd have to let my real feelings show on my face. That in itself terrified me.

I felt a rush of breath escape when I walked into the room. Jade had her back to me, her head down, as she pushed down the feet of some poor soul doing leg lifts. I could faintly hear her counting above the din of noise in the crowded gym.

"You really need to stretch out today. You haven't been here in a while," Miranda reminded me.

I went to work on my legs, trying to keep my eyes on the mat, but they betrayed me, and my gaze drifted to the mirror, and there it met Jade's. Her brow was furrowed as she slowly nodded at me. I couldn't control the muscles in my face. I had no idea what my expression looked like, but I mouthed a silent "thanks," and she nodded again. It was her place of work; she didn't have any choice but to be there, but I did. That she let me return meant a lot.

It was lower body night, and after Miranda and I finished our cardio, we moved to the leg presses. I had done a pretty good job of not looking at Jade, but I could sense her gaze upon me. I was on my stomach hoisting the weights nearly to my backside. They seemed heavier than before, but I figured that since I'd been away for a while that it would take more exertion.

What I had failed to realize was that I had not checked the weight. It dawned on me that the reason I was having so much trouble was because I was lifting too much. That thought was going through my head when the muscle in the back of my right thigh felt like it was curling into a ball. I let out a groan, maybe a squeal, and rolled onto the floor.

I was writhing when Miranda squatted beside me. "What's going on?"

"I think I pulled something," I grunted out breathlessly.

I heard Jade's voice then. "Don't touch her. She doesn't like to be touched."

I looked up, and she had her arms spread, keeping the other trainers from getting to me. The crowd around us was looking at Jade and Miranda like they were callous assholes for not helping me. "She's right, let me just breathe for a minute," I said between clenched teeth.

"Sloan, try to stretch that leg out," Jade said. I could hear the stress in her voice. "Pull it back toward your shoulder."

I was in so much pain, I could barely lift it. Miranda grabbed me by the ankle and gently pushed. The relief was such a surprise, and I was so lost in it that the images stayed just at the edge of my mind's eye. I felt her anxiety and sympathy, though.

I looked past Miranda at Jade, and I could see the perplexed expression on her face. Miranda was touching me, and I was certain that mystified her. Her brow relaxed, and her head cocked slightly to the side. Something I couldn't decipher passed over her face for a fleeting second. Her eyes met mine. "Do you feel relief?"

"Yes," I pushed out breathlessly. "But it feels like if she lets go that it will ball up again."

"You need to stand. Miranda, slowly lower her leg and see if you can get her up," Jade said.

When Miranda released me, I felt the muscle coiling back, and I rolled onto my stomach, gasping. She looped her arms under my shoulders and tried to pull me. I was in such a hurry to get up that my left foot kept sliding from beneath me. I couldn't stop the whimpers that were preceding a full-blown cry.

Miranda released me, and I felt two sets of hands reach under my arms. The pain was so intense, it was still at the forefront of my mind. Emotions felt like they were hitting me on both sides of my body. To my right was compassion and empathy. I knew that was Miranda. To my left, the same, but tinged with fear and the knowledge that she couldn't stand to see me hurt, and I knew it was Jade.

They walked me over to the wall where I put my hands and straightened my legs. I felt their touch slip away and my emotions return. "Thank you both," I rasped out. Not caring who was standing around, I said, "I know what you risked to help me."

Jade's voice was tremulous. "You need to go home and get off that leg. Ice and elevate it as soon as you can, okay?"

Miranda walked me to her car and helped me inside. I had to leave my mine behind. There was no way I could work the clutch. "Spend the night with me. You were coming over anyway. We'll get your car in the morning."

I pushed hard against the floor board to keep the muscle in my leg from contacting. Miranda climbed into the driver's side and drove slowly. "I couldn't get into your mind. The pain was so bad, I couldn't have done it if I had wanted to."

"Jade was touching you, too. Was it the same with her?"

"Yeah, but I felt both of your emotions. I could feel sympathy coming from both sides."

"That's something." Miranda's fingers tapped out a rhythm on the steering wheel. "I wonder if intense arousal would have the same effect," she said with a smile.

"She touched me knowing what could happen, but she did it anyway because I was hurting."

The smile slipped from Miranda's face. "She could've asked one of the other trainers to do it, but she didn't. She was willing to sacrifice her privacy for you."

Neither of us said anything for the rest of the drive home. Unlike Miranda, I had an idea of what Jade had faced in life and how badly she wanted to keep it hidden. She cared enough about me to help when I needed her, and that was all I needed to know.

I was lying on Miranda's couch with my leg propped up and an ice pack strapped to my thigh as Miranda told Marty about our harrowing adventure.

"Oh, you poor baby." Marty reached out to stroke my hair.

I saw Miranda grab her hand. "Don't do that."

Marty seemed to remember the bullshit story that Miranda had told everyone, but it was obvious she was perturbed.

"I need to talk to you, Marty," I began. She took a seat in my line of vision with an attentive expression. "It's about my experience, but I want you to keep what I tell you between us."

"That goes without saying, honey. Unless I have your express permission, I never disclose what we discuss."

"Well, you may be tempted with this because it's a doozy." Miranda said, "What?" when I glared at her.

"Something about me changed when I woke up...when I touch people, I can see their memories like I'm living them myself." Marty looked at Miranda first as if she expected her to burst out laughing at any moment, then back at me. "I'm not jerking your chain."

"Touch me then." She looked at me with the same unbelieving expression that Miranda had given when I first told her as she thrust out her hand far enough for me to reach it. I looked back at Miranda.

"Do it," Miranda said with a nod. "She won't believe any other way."

I took Marty's hand. I was sitting at her desk staring at the computer screen. Frustration coursed through me like lightning. I felt threatened because my coworkers seemed to be catching on much faster than me. I had a pencil in my mouth and spit out the eraser that I'd bitten off in disgust. I needed comfort, so I opened the right drawer of my desk and rifled around until I found the Milky Way I'd hidden under a stack of manila envelopes.

The connection broke when Marty pulled her hand away. She looked at me expectantly with a grin that slid from her face as I began to tell what I'd seen and felt.

"That's a pretty elaborate prank," Marty said, looking at us. "Who in my office did you enlist to help with it?" Her tone was slightly biting.

"Touch her again," Miranda said, looking at Marty. "Give her another shot."

Marty sighed and held out her hand again. The moment I touched her, I felt her resentment at being the butt of what she thought was a joke. Her stress about the new program and her ability to learn it sat at the forefront of her mind. I relaxed and felt myself go deeper. I felt like I had a remote in my hand, and I was changing stations on a TV for something personal that did not include Miranda.

I recognized Marty's mother. She was sitting in a chair with a tissue dabbing at her eyes. She looked so young. Marty looked down at the portion of her legs that her gown didn't cover. The paper of the examination table crinkled in her hands as she squeezed it. I heard another woman talking, but I only caught bits and pieces. I realized that was all Marty was able to hear as her mind raced. "Ectopic pregnancy, damage to fallopian tubes, getting pregnant again would be difficult." Relief and sadness washed through her at the same time.

Marty broke the connection again and stood. "If you two are finished screwing with me, I'm going to start dinner."

"Wait." Miranda looked at me. "Tell her what you saw."

I shook my head. Miranda had never told me that Marty had gotten pregnant, maybe she didn't know.

"Tell her," Miranda implored.

"Yes, tell me," Marty said with a hand on her hip.

"You lost the baby," I blurted out without any tact.

Marty's hand slipped from her hip and dangled against her thigh. "What did you say?"

Miranda shot up off the couch, her eyes fixed on Marty.

This wasn't going well, and I wanted to take it all back. "I'm sorry."

"When were you pregnant?" Miranda demanded.

Marty stared at me with anger and shock. "You tell me," she said with a challenging tone.

"Your mom looked to be very young, so I'm guessing maybe high school. The doctor was female, but you never looked at her, so I didn't see her face. She said the pregnancy had been ectopic, and there was damage…you might have trouble conceiving again."

Marty's mouth dropped wider and wider as I spoke. She was gaping at me. I almost felt the urge to jump up and run, throbbing leg and all.

"Why didn't you tell me about this?" Miranda asked a bit more calmly.

Marty turned her head slowly toward Miranda. "I was fifteen and too curious for my own good." Her tone was dreamy when she spoke. "No one knew but me, Mom, and my doctor."

"I shouldn't have told that," I said, feeling horrible. "I… couldn't make you believe if it was something everyone else already knew. I'm so sorry, Marty. I should've let you go on believing we were joking."

"Sloan…" Marty took a step back and sat down. "This is real?"

I nodded as she tried to wrap her brain around it. "I can't help it…well, I'm trying to. Miranda's been working with me. But if someone touches me and I can't always make myself stop, I see their innermost secrets."

"That's why we went to Deb. Sloan saw that she had an eating disorder when they bumped in the kitchen," Miranda said, seeming to put the revelation of the pregnancy out of her mind for a moment.

"You…" Marty rubbed at her brow. "That's the real reason we couldn't touch you?"

"I didn't want to invade your minds. I have to keep my distance for the sake of your privacy and my sanity."

Marty cupped her hands over her mouth and sat back. The wheels of her mind were spinning behind her eyes.

We all talked for a while. Dinner was forgotten, but none of us was hungry. I knew they needed time to talk alone, so I told them I was tired. As I stood awkwardly, Marty walked over. It was clear she intended to hug me, but I stopped her. "We can't," I said sadly. "I still haven't mastered blocking the images, and I'm afraid of what I'll take from you."

Marty's arms dropped to her sides. "I'm so sorry."

I smiled. "One day, I'll be able to accept that hug. Save it for me."

She blew me a kiss. "I will."

Chapter 13

Miranda and I skipped going to the health club the following night. She and Marty needed some time together. The night after that, Miranda was at work, so we didn't go then, either. I wanted to see Jade, but I knew better than to go there by myself. Unattended, I was nothing but trouble, so I waited on my keeper.

I wasn't sure how to play it with Jade when we walked into the health club, so I caught her eye and did that nod thing we do. The gym wasn't very crowded because of the thunderstorm that moved in right at rush hour. As a result, I could hear Jade's voice more than usual. I listened to her count and encourage. I liked the sound of it and hoped I'd hear it again in conversation with me.

Miranda was unusually quiet, and I asked her if things were okay at home.

"We've done a lot of talking and soul-searching since your visit," she said. "That's not a bad thing, so don't think you've wrecked my marriage. If anything, it did us a lot of good. We talked like we used to in our first year together. I guess I didn't realize how much we've drifted because of the mundane things." She grinned, showing me all her teeth. "And the sex has been fantastic. I'm exhausted."

"I'm happy for you." I truly was, but a tiny sprig of jealousy sprung up somewhere deep within. I guess envy would've been a better description. I looked over at Jade and was surprised to find myself wondering if we'd ever have talks like that.

Miranda and I got separated while we went through our circuit of machines. I took the time to hydrate myself and stood off in the corner. Jade made a move toward me, and I felt encouraged.

"How're you feeling?" She walked up and folded her arms.

"Better. Thank you for your help the other night."

She shrugged it off. "It's part of my job."

"You touched me," I said, lowering my voice, "knowing the consequences. I'd say that's above and beyond your job. I didn't see anything. I was hurting too bad," I said because I knew she wanted to ask.

"I can't tell you how exposed…naked I feel around you," she said without looking at me.

"Would it make you feel better if I stripped off my clothes?"

"No." She didn't laugh or even smile at my attempt at levity.

"Sorry, Jade, I can only imagine how uncomfortable you must feel around me. I regret not being upfront."

"I know you weren't withholding for nosy reasons. I've tried to put myself in your shoes, and I think I might've been the same way." She sighed. "Still it doesn't make it any easier."

It bothered me that she wouldn't look at me when we talked. "I have an idea. Why don't we talk on the phone? If you want to, of course. I'll answer anything you want to ask."

She thought about it for a minute or two as she watched her next client come through the door. "I have to go, but…I'll call you."

"Okay," I said as she walked away.

Miranda and I slipped back into our routine when she was off during the day. I had truly become a lab rat to her, and she experimented every chance she got. One time, she scared the shit out of me when she jumped out of a corner and screamed. I was so shaken, I didn't realize she had a hold of my arms. Another time, she pinched me on the soft part of my arm above my elbow. I was so focused on the stinging that I didn't realize she'd pressed her leg to mine. Then came the tickling. She had me backed into a corner, making me squeal and scream, when a customer walked in.

On my lunch breaks, she'd make me close my eyes and focus on something, and she'd touch me. I was able to force down the images that came as long as I stayed focused. After a week, she'd walk up and touch me while I was working, and I was overjoyed to realize that the rejection of her thoughts was becoming second nature.

One evening, I joined her and Marty for dinner, and while I was eating, Marty laid her hand on my arm. I concentrated on the food, the taste, and texture and was able to keep myself centered. Miranda and I agreed that I'd passed a milestone. I was high on my success and was about to turn in for the night when the phone rang after nine thirty. My heart skipped a beat when I heard Jade's voice.

"I'm sorry it's so late. Would you prefer me to call you on the weekend?" she said when I picked up.

I answered honestly. "If you had called me at four in the morning, I would've been just as happy to hear from you."

"Why?"

"Because it gives me hope."

She was silent, and I could hear Guy meowing and food hitting his bowl. "What are you going to use this ability for?"

I was taken aback by the question. "I've never really thought about using it. I spend more time trying to silence it."

"I suppose some would use it to cash in. In the wrong hands, it could be a powerful blackmail tool."

I thought about Jacquelyn Marlow and how dirty I felt after leaving her mind. "I'm human and I have my weaknesses and faults, but I can honestly say that has never crossed my mind. It's more of a handicap than a bonus."

"How long after your accident did you realize you had this... thing?"

I felt like I was being interviewed and my answers were of the utmost importance. "I think I noticed it when my friend Deb hugged me. I thought I was high on something they gave me in the hospital. But it continued to happen, and I realized I was actually seeing things...things that we both remembered but in the perspective of my friends."

"Miranda told me it took you two months to confide in her. It must've been hard to cope with alone."

"It was. I thought I was going crazy. I don't think I had ever felt more isolated in my life. My childhood should've prepared me for that, but I was so…lonely."

She went quiet again. "I think I'd like to hear about your childhood…if you want to tell me."

"Jade, you know what I've taken from you. I think it's fair that you be able to ask anything you want to know."

"You make it sound like you've intentionally stolen something from me. Is that how you feel?"

"Yeah, I do. I didn't mean to see the things I saw." I winced. "But…I did."

"Is that why you want to talk to me? You feel guilty?"

"No," I said immediately.

"Tell me about your childhood if you don't mind."

I rambled for a while about the death of my mother and being stuck with an aunt who clearly didn't want me or my brother. I was careful not to whine or make it appear I wanted her sympathy. Jade was no stranger to loneliness; I could feel it the few times we touched. I just wanted her to understand that because of my past I might be able to relate to her. Though she didn't make a sound, I was pretty certain she was listening to everything intently. When I finished talking, I heard Guy meowing his head off. "Is he okay?"

"He's complaining about something." I could hear Jade moving around, then I heard, "Oh…yuck."

"Did he get sick?"

"No, but I might be. One of my clients is a cat lover, so she's been teaching me all about them. She says they like to give gifts, and I think I might've gotten my first."

I could still hear Guy yowling. "I'm afraid to ask."

"It's a lizard, or part of one, anyway. It must've come through the open window. I think he's telling me to go ahead and take a bite."

"Well, that's sweet…in a gross sort of way."

Jade laughed. "Do you think he'd be offended if I flushed it?"

"Maybe you should pretend to eat it."

Jade sounded disgusted. "I hope *you* won't be offended if I don't ask your opinion on such things in the future." She accented her point by flushing the toilet.

"I'm totally inept in that department, which should be fairly obvious now."

"So tell me about what you do. What kind of store do you have?"

I could hear her settling down again, and I figured Guy was very close because I could hear his purring.

I told her about the store and its contents. "I like the idea of people being able to bring home some of the sea."

"I like the beach here, but it's not what I expected when I pictured Florida. It's really murky and muddy," Jade said.

"You've been to Alligator Point then."

"Yeah, I was afraid to go in."

"There's a river that empties into the Gulf nearby that makes the water pretty funky looking. But if you would've passed the turn-off to Alligator Point and continued on that highway, you'd see the beaches you're looking for. St. George Island is one of my favorite places to go."

"I've explored the area some, but I'm afraid to stray too far. My truck isn't all that reliable."

The notion hit me fast and flew straight out of my mouth. "I could take you sometime. I know the area really well, and I love to cruise the coast."

"If you promise to keep your hands to yourself."

I wanted to laugh until I realized it wasn't a joke. "I won't touch you without your permission."

She was quiet for a second. "Do you think you'll ever be able to control it?"

"If you would've asked me that a few weeks ago, I would've said no. But Miranda works with me nearly every day, and I'm learning. Most days, it feels like my brain is splitting in half. But I had dinner with Miranda and her partner, Marty, tonight and Marty touched me while we were eating. I stopped myself before going into her mind. It's slowly becoming instinct to block the images when I come in contact with someone."

"The night you told me your secret, you said you feel emotions. Is that something you've learned to control, as well?"

I swallowed hard and hoped that my answer would not set us back. "No, I can't control that. The only way I know how to describe it is to compare it with electricity, it just flows. Whoever I touch, their feelings become mine." I took a deep breath and dared to continue. "The night at the gym when I pulled the muscle in my thigh, I felt your compassion and your fear."

"Hmm…"

My palm started to sweat. I rubbed it on my shirt and waited.

"I guess shaking hands with someone might be a double-edged sword. I think if I were you, I'd stick to the germaphobe thing."

"Was…was that an attempt at levity?"

Jade's response was more than a chuckle. "I'm working until noon Saturday. Are you off?"

"I will be as soon as I call Kaylie. She's my part-time help."

"Okay."

The slight exhale after "okay" said what Jade didn't—"I'll give you another chance."

"Great, I'll pick you up at noon then."

Chapter 14

"I'm excited and scared for you," Miranda said after I told her about my weekend plans. "You have an opportunity here. You can't screw it up."

"I've been telling myself that since I talked to Jade."

I was bent over straightening a row of hand-carved dolphins crafted from driftwood when Miranda pinched me hard on the ass. "Ow, shit! Damn it, Miranda!"

She grinned, and her gaze darted to her hand on my arm. "Focus, don't go there."

"Okay, I think we've conquered shock and ow, so you can stop torturing me."

She steepled her fingers together and bowed at the waist. "I think you are ready for your first test, grasshopper."

"Yes, I'm sure I'll do fine if Jade punches me in the jaw." I went back to work, and out of the corner of my eye, I saw Miranda pick up a boat paddle. "If you hit me with that, I swear I will break everything in this store over your head."

Miranda looked disappointed as she replaced the paddle. "So you still feel our emotions, but you can stop the memories from flowing into your mind."

I watched her warily as she moved along the aisles. "That's right."

"What are you going to do if things really begin to heat up with Jade and she lets you do something crazy like hold her hand? Are you going to be upfront first and tell her that you'll sense her emotions?"

"I think hand-holding is a bit ambitious, don't you think? And

I've already told her about the emotion thing. She didn't seem to be rattled. Given our history, I don't think she'll be letting me touch her anytime soon."

"Sloan, she likes you, and you like her. This relationship is bound to get physical. Let's experiment. Hold my hand while you work."

"I'm not going to hold your hand. I nearly lost a customer the other day when you had your tickle fest."

"If someone comes in, we'll let go." Miranda held out her hand. "I'm serious, take it."

"No." I turned around and walked off. She met me on the next aisle. "You can't experiment on her. Take my damn hand."

I huffed and took it. We stood there staring at each other with our hands locked. "I feel so stupid, and your fingers are sticky."

"Ah!" Miranda held up a finger on her free hand. "See, it's working. You're focused on how dumb you feel. Now if you took Jade's hand, you could focus on the feel of how great it was to connect with her."

I felt a grin tugging at my lips. "You're right. You're a sticky pain in the ass, but you're right, and I love you for it." I squeezed her hand tightly in mine and reveled in the warmth of it.

On Saturday morning, I sprang out of bed like a kid on Christmas Day. I sang in the shower and dressed with lightning speed. I had visions of Jade and me flying down the highway with our hair blowing in the breeze, and I couldn't wait. With my sunglasses poised on top of my head and a bag full of towels and sunscreen hanging on my shoulder, I looked up at the clock—it was only ten. "Aw, shit." I had no idea what I was going to do for the next two hours.

Promptly at noon, I pulled into the gym parking lot and waited. Jade emerged five minutes later wearing a tank top and a pair of red board shorts. She was grinning from ear to ear, and so was I.

"I love this car," she said as she climbed in.

"I'll let you drive it if you want, but you won't be able to look at it as much."

She seemed to consider the offer for a minute and declined.

We rolled the windows down, and a warm wind filled the car. Over the noise, Jade told me about her morning and the latest gift that Guy had given her—a half-eaten moth on her bed. But when we began down the coast, she quieted.

I glanced her way a few times, and her gaze was fixed on the water through my window. Every now and then, she'd comment on something she saw like a fish jumping or a piece of driftwood caught on a sandbar. And she'd smile a genuine smile that transformed her face and let me know she was truly enjoying herself.

Miranda and I had made this trip often, and as close as we were, she didn't seem to enjoy it like I did. The beauty of the water slipping behind groves of trees only to reappear again in all its glory failed to take her breath away like it did mine. It did for Jade, though. I watched her as often as I could and took great pleasure at how her eyes would widen or how she'd exclaim when she noticed a dolphin.

I sank lower in my seat, so she could have a full view of something that had always been a precious wonder to me. The slow realization swept over me like the tide as it moved the water to the beach. I wasn't planning my next move, nor did I wonder what the end of the day would bring. I was perfectly content to embrace every second, every sight, and savor the blissful connection with Jade as we shared something we loved.

"Can we stop and walk out on one of those sandbars?" she asked.

"Um, there's an old hotel just up ahead. We can use their parking lot and hike back a little ways."

"You mind doing that?" Jade stared through my window.

"Not at all," I said with a grin. I glanced back at her, and her gaze was set upon me. She looked pleased and extremely happy.

I parked and we walked through the brush until we could get onto the sand. One of the things I appreciated about this stretch of road was that the highway department saw fit to leave the thickets.

It made me feel like the area was wild and untamed, waiting to be explored. The narrow slip of beach widened, and we took off our shoes to feel the sand beneath our feet. Jade was like a child and raced past me to the sandbar she'd spotted. In some places, it was submerged in a foot of water, and she would wade across it to get to one shell or another.

"Beach rules are you can keep a shell if it's uninhabited." Jade looked back at me in question as a tiny claw reached out and brushed her finger. I laughed as she jumped and dropped it into the water. "That was a hermit crab. He was saying hello."

"I think it was more like 'unhand my house.'" Jade and I watched the little claws come of out the shell and move it farther away. "Do they pinch hard?"

I reached down and picked the shell up again, and the crab disappeared inside. "No, but the larger crabs do. If you hold this guy real still, he'll come back out." I demonstrated, and we watched as his face and claws reappeared.

"You think I gave him a head injury or something when I dropped him?" Jade asked, wrinkling her nose.

"Nah, he hit the water. He probably sees more action when he gets rolled by a big wave."

"What makes you think it's a guy?" Jade asked.

"Look at his shell." I pointed to the barnacles. "A woman wouldn't get caught dead in this, and she certainly wouldn't wear white before Easter."

Jade smiled and wrinkled her nose at my dumb joke.

After Jade had thoroughly investigated the sandbar and collected more shells than we both could carry, we went back to the car and deposited them in the trunk. I figured by the end of the day, it would smell like a dead mermaid.

We passed the road to St. George Island after I assured Jade we'd come back and explore it. I wanted her to see Apalachicola, a quaint seaside town with a strip of shops and restaurants. As we climbed from the car, seagulls flew overhead and reminded us that we were still near the water. "You should be hungry by now," I said as I walked alongside Jade.

"I'm always hungry, remember?"

"Good, I know just the place." I led her to a restaurant and requested to be seated on the balcony. I watched Jade's face as she read over the menu. She was more relaxed than I'd ever seen her. She'd smile as she looked over the railing at something below, then sip her tea and go back to the menu. We both decided on the seafood bisque and salads.

"I assume you eat the same way you've instructed Miranda and me to eat," I said when the waiter departed.

"I do as a matter of habit."

"Do you ever break that habit?"

Jade tilted her head to the side. "I think you're about to propose something bad."

"There's a store that has a soda fountain. They make marvelous root beer floats."

"Well, technically, I'm not your trainer. But even if I was, I'd have to say that a root beer float every now and then is a good thing."

I grinned. "Then save room for dessert."

Jade's focus became solely on me. "Thank you for taking me on this adventure. I can't remember when I've had so much fun. I get caught up on my hamster wheel. Home, work, grocery store, repeat."

"I know exactly what you mean. I try to make a trip like this once a month."

"Ah, so this is how you romanced your women." Jade raised a brow.

"You find this romantic?" I asked, afraid that I was treading on thin ice, no pun.

"Very," Jade said with a nod. "Dinner and a movie can't compare to this."

"I know it's going to disappoint you to hear that I come…alone."

Jade grinned. "You're lying."

I wagged a finger at her. "I gave you my word I wouldn't do that. I do make this trip alone, and I do it often."

"Okay, so you haven't brought *all* your women here."

I shook my head. "The only other woman that's made this trip with me is Miranda."

"What did I do to rank such special treatment?" she asked lightly.

"I don't think you believe me when I tell you that I really like you." I met her gaze.

Her expression turned serious. "What exactly do you like about me?"

"You're compassionate and caring, even though you haven't been on the receiving end of that very often." I paused, hoping I hadn't said too much, but she looked receptive. "I can't really explain why I'm so drawn to you, but it's not just your looks. There's just something special about you, and I want to know more."

Jade opened her mouth to say something when the waiter appeared with our salads. I tried to gauge how she was feeling, but her expression was unreadable. We ate for a few minutes in silence before she picked the conversation back up. "I like you too, Sloan. We've had a rough start, and I have to thank Miranda for jumping in and explaining a lot that I didn't understand." She looked embarrassed. "I could've let you explain, but I felt like I was made of glass the night you told me what you were able to do."

"Can we make a deal?" I set my fork down. She looked at me in question. "For now, can we stop analyzing why we like each other and just accept it as so?"

"Deal." She reached over with her fork, and I picked mine up and tapped it against hers. "That's as good as a pinky swear," I said with a laugh.

We strolled down the street window shopping. Jade had an eye for the unique, and if she thought she could, she would've dragged me into what looked like an old warehouse. Instead, she waved me on to quickly follow her long stride. When we entered the building, we both let out a long sigh. "This place is so cool," I said. "I never noticed it on my visits." If it had been on a boat or a ship, it was there.

Jade was running her hand over an old maritime chart when I walked up.

"Do you know how to read these by any chance?"

"No, do you?"

"Nope, but they really are cool to look at."

"Look at these." Jade picked up a flag from a box. "There's hundreds of them here from boats and ships. They're kind of worn. They must've really been used." She ran her fingers over the fabric. "Can you imagine all the places they've been?"

"Look at this." I pointed to a plaque. "I think this was taken from the actual vessel. The plaque read "Lady Corrine." "I'll bet this would look great in your apartment."

Jade looked at it for a moment. "That was my grandmother's name. I was named after her," she said dreamily.

"Would you like to have it?"

Jade shook her head with a smile. "Nah, it's a want, not a need."

She walked off, so I took it down and tucked it under my arm. We parted as she moved deeper into the store looking at the shells in the back. I made a quick trip to the register and paid for the plaque and asked the clerk to hold it at the counter for me while I looked around.

We met up again at a counter covered in packages of fishnets. "You like these?" I asked.

"Yeah, I could hang it in the corner of my living room and put all my shells in it."

"I have tons of these at my store. I ordered them when I first opened, and I think I may've sold a dozen. I'd be happy to give you as many as you want."

"I'll buy a couple. I want to see your store, and it'll give me a good excuse to come by."

"You don't need an excuse," I said softly as she walked away.

"What'd you buy?" she asked when we walked out.

"Can't tell you, it's a secret." I grinned at her when she frowned. "I might let you in on it after a root beer float."

We meandered toward the soda fountain...well, I did. Jade darted from one window front to the next, taking in everything.

When we got to the shop I was looking for, I held the door open, and Jade walked through with a grin. She looked at all the old candies and toys, running her fingers over everything. "It's like being in a Norman Rockwell painting."

"It does make you feel like you've gone back in time, at least until you get to the back of the shop where the souvenirs are."

The place was kind of crowded, so we got our floats to go. We'd circled the strip twice before we decided to head to St. George Island. This time, Jade accepted my offer and took the wheel. She let out a yell when I told her to stomp it and she did.

"Do you think it's funny that you and Miranda both turned out to be gay?" she asked when we were flying down the highway again.

"Not really. I think we both recognized a kindred spirit when we met and became friends." I shook my head and laughed at the memory. "I took one look at her cut-off shorts and football jersey, and I knew she would be fun."

"Was there ever a romantic connection?"

"Oh, no, we became sisters, and that was never a notion in our heads. I think she recognized her sexuality first. Miranda is the introspective, analytical one. We realized that we were on the same page one day when we admitted to having crushes on Abigail Royce, the queen of rebellion at our school. I think we were around fifteen then."

I took the opportunity to study Jade as she drove, pretending to be looking out her window. She looked better, cooler behind the wheel than I did, even though she was having some difficulty managing the sparse leg room. "How old were you when you realized you were?"

"Around fifth grade, I guess. I was so tall, and the girls were always trying to climb on me like I was a tree. I realized one day that I really liked it." Jade shook her head as her hair whirled around her face. "It blossomed after that, I suppose."

"How old were you when you had your first kiss?" I pushed. Jade liked to ask questions but didn't appear too hip on answering. At first, I assumed it was me, but I began to wonder if she did the same thing with everyone.

"Seventeen." She didn't comment further nor did she ask me anything else, so I decided to be quiet and enjoy the ride. It wasn't until we started across the long bridge to the island that she spoke again. "How old were you?"

The question took me by surprise since the conversation had dropped. "I was fifteen, and Abigail Royce taught me a thing or two about kissing. Wow, was that a bone of contention between Miranda and me for a while, but we got over it." I took advantage of the opportunity and asked another question. "How do your parents handle your sexuality? Accepting, or is it still an elephant in the room?"

Jade's eyes remained on the road. "They're dead," she said without any emotion.

"I'm sorry." I waited for her to tell me it was a car accident or plane crash, something that took them both at the same time, but she didn't say a word until I offered to take the wheel back, so she could see the island. It was odd to me that she didn't mention it when I told her about losing my mother. The thought struck me that it might've happened recently and was too raw and painful to discuss.

"I can't imagine living in a place like this," Jade said as she watched the beach houses go by. "I would think I was in heaven."

"I fantasize about it when I come here, but Panacea for now is as close as I'm going to get."

I pulled up at the gate to the entrance of the state park that took up one end of the island and paid for a day pass. I looked at Jade when we started to move again. "You like to camp?"

"No." Jade shook her head and looked out her window. "There was a time I did it a lot and burned out."

"I asked because there's a campground here, and I was going to show you the spur if you were interested." She shook her head and continued to stare at the sand dunes as we drove by.

Fortunately, the water was still chilly, and that kept the crowds away. There were only a half-dozen cars in the lot at the beach access when I pulled in. "Wanna have a look at the beach?"

"Yes," Jade said enthusiastically.

I popped the trunk and grabbed a plastic bag in case Jade found more shells. The trunk was ripe. I suspected that we might've found an inhabited shell, but none was moving. I hoped the creature had already given up the ghost when we grabbed the shell. I coughed and slammed the trunk, mentally adding Febreze to my shopping list.

"This is what I pictured Florida to look like," Jade said as the water came into view.

Waves pounded the sandy shore in the afternoon light, and I felt light as a feather as I walked by her side down the wooden bridge. "The water in the Keys is even prettier, but this is still so…"

"Peaceful and invigorating at the same time," Jade said. "Magical."

I smiled. "Exactly." We walked down to the water's edge and let it lap at our ankles. "I brought towels in case you wanted to brave it and go in. It's still too cold for me, though."

"Do you mind if we just walk?"

"So you can collect shells?" I said with a grin.

"Maybe just a few," she said with a shrug, "hundred."

"We're gonna need more bags, maybe a wheelbarrow."

"I'll go easy on you this time." She bent down and gathered up two. "Next time, bring the wheelbarrow."

"Ah! You said next time. Does that mean you'll do this with me again?"

She dropped the shells into the bag. "As long as you want my company."

I took that as a good sign.

We were so absorbed in shell collecting and sightseeing that neither of us had paid attention to how far we'd walked until she turned and noticed that the boardwalk looked like a dot on the horizon. "I guess we should turn around," Jade said with disappointment in her voice. "It's getting late. I saw a sign that said the park closes at dark."

"That's okay. We have enough daylight to get back, plus we get to see the show."

She looked at me in question.

"We get to watch the sunset on our walk."

She looked at me for a long moment and smiled. "Thank you again for sharing this with me."

I could smell the sea and Jade's sweet scent intermingled. It moved over my skin like a caress. We wouldn't hold hands on the walk back. There would be no kiss good night, but in that moment with her standing there smiling at me backlit by the setting sun, it was enough. We had connected, and it was sweeter and more exciting than any encounter I'd ever had.

Chapter 15

My headlights illuminated Jade's truck. I hated the thought of separating. We could've sat in that parking lot and looked at the stars all night without saying a word, and I would've been thrilled.

"Sloan," Jade said softly. "Do you…consider this a date?"

"I would love to think of it that way, but if friendship is all you have to offer, I'll take it."

A smiled played at the corners of her mouth, then her expression turned serious. "Do you honestly think you'll be able…to touch without…"

"I've come a long way. I feel pretty safe in saying that I could touch your hand right now and stay in control, but it's going to come down to you trusting me. I'm willing to wait for as long as that takes."

She stared down at her hand in her lap. I held my breath as she slowly raised it. She was staring deep into my eyes as I lifted my hand. They were a breath apart, and I could feel the heat radiating off her palm.

If someone had told me a year before that I would be sitting in my car waiting for a woman to simply touch my hand, I would've laughed. But in that moment, I wanted nothing more to feel her hand against mine. Jade slowly let her palm rest against mine. I smiled and felt her fingers clasp the back of my hand. We sat there for a long moment just looking at each other until she released me.

"Thank you," I said on a sigh.

"What did you focus on to keep your mind occupied?"

"Your eyes and the softness of your skin."

She climbed out of the car and leaned into the window. "I think that…was sweeter than a kiss."

And then she was gone.

"I thought you didn't like holding my hand."

"I love you, but I really don't." I held her hand tightly in mine as I dragged Miranda with me while we restocked my shelves.

"I can't believe she trusted you enough to touch hands on the first date," Miranda said seriously.

I straightened and grinned. "That sounds so…antiquated."

"But it's monumental for you and Jade." Miranda scratched the back of her neck with her free hand. "I spent the whole day wondering what it would be like if Marty had your thing. Since the night you let her cat out of the bag, we've been really open, but if she could do what you do, I wonder what she could pull from my mind and what she'd think. Would she be disappointed in me knowing that I cheated on my emergency medical tech exam?"

"You did?"

Miranda nodded slowly. "Somebody gave me an old copy of the written portion of the test, and I used it as a study guide. That's cheating."

"Well, it wasn't the actual test."

"Rationalize how you want to. In my heart, I cheated."

I shook my head. "You had perfect scores all through that course. You could've passed that test with your eyes closed."

Miranda raised her free hand and let it drop. "Anxiety. Anyway, my point is that you're gonna have to be very careful to build Jade's trust. From what you told me about your date, she took a big step."

"Yeah, she did," I said with a nod. "She told me that it was sweeter than a kiss. It was. I've gone on dates, and the next time we went out, we were in bed. I've gone from that to being excited about the touch of her hand in mine." I took a step toward the storeroom and Miranda planted her feet. I turned and looked when she wouldn't budge. "What?"

"I don't think I've ever seen you look like you do now. It sounds trite, but you're kinda glowing."

"Now you're embarrassing me." I tried to shake my hand loose, but Miranda tightened her grip.

"You're so cute," she said with a laugh.

"Feel free to stop right now."

She tugged her cell phone out of her pocket. "I'm gonna take a picture."

"Let me go." I twisted my hand, jerked it free, and took off.

Miranda chased me through the store yelling, "Hold still."

I was laughing like a fool when I came face to face with Jade. She looked at me, then Miranda, who was still staring at her camera. "Pose for me, little lovebird. You know you want…uh, hey, Jade."

"Hey, Miranda," she said with an amused smile. "Am I interrupting training?"

"Nah, she's getting ready to graduate, and I wanted to take her picture."

I stuck my hands in the back pockets of my jeans to resist touching her. "Actually, you just saved me from being tormented. How'd you get away from the gym?"

"One of my clients didn't show, so I scored a very short lunch break. I wanted to buy a couple of those fishnets for my shells."

"Oh, they're over here, come see." She followed me to the shelf, and I pulled out a few. "Some are colored and some aren't. Those look more real to me."

"Hey," Miranda said, causing Jade and me to look at her. I heard the shutter sound her phone made when it took a picture. "I'll send you both a copy." I glared at Miranda, and she turned and went toward the counter. "It's a cute picture."

Jade looked back at me, and I rolled my eyes, "She's insane. It's one of the reasons I love her."

Jade laughed and pointed to one of the nets in my hands. "I think I like the ones without color. I'll take two, but I'm buying them."

I lowered my voice, so Miranda couldn't hear and invariably comment. "Since we're dating, they're a gift."

"If you feel that way about it, I want the wicker chair in the corner," Jade said softly with a smile.

"It's yours. I'll have Miranda load it into the back of your truck."

"I was joking."

"You should tell her you want the matching sofa," Miranda called out. "But it's gonna take all three of us to load it."

Jade laughed out loud. "Just the nets, and I can load those myself."

"I know you're always hungry. Want to come out back and have lunch?" I asked.

"I can't." Jade looked at her watch. "I'd really love to, but I can't stay that long."

"How about a doggie bag? She's gonna make me eat a casserole that's been in her fridge for two days. I'd like to get rid of it. Thank God, I have to go back to work tomorrow," Miranda called out again.

I leaned in close but kept from touching Jade. "I wouldn't do that to you."

"You suck, Sloan," Miranda said.

"Shut up, you." I looked at Jade again. "I made fresh chicken salad this morning. Two stray cats ate the rest of the casserole. Would you like a sandwich to eat on the way?"

"Since you insist."

"I do." It was the most natural thing in the world to put my hand out for her to take. She hesitated, and I realized what I'd done. I tried to pull it back when she grabbed it. "Thanks for trusting me," I said with a smile that she returned.

Miranda's jaw sagged when we rounded the corner, then she clapped. "Oh, you really did graduate today."

"Come on, I have chicken salad," I said to her with a grin. She fell in step behind us.

I sent Jade back to work with a sandwich, chips, and a bottle of water. She was thrilled, and so was I.

"I cannot believe you held her hand, and she let you!" Miranda exclaimed.

"Me either." We jumped around my kitchen like two kids who had just been told they were going to Disney World.

Miranda scrubbed her face with both hands. "That was worth you holding my hand all morning. Now the next step is the kiss."

"I'm not kissing you, don't worry."

"Oh, come on." Miranda puckered her lips as she walked toward me. "It's for science."

I ran.

I had a shipment arrive late at the store, and by the time everything was moved into the storeroom, our gym time was gone. Even though I got to see Jade a little while at lunch, I was disappointed. Miranda took pity on me and suggested we go anyway, but I knew Marty was waiting on her and I was hungry.

I'd bought a couple of steaks I intended to grill for Miranda and me. As I stood staring into the fridge, an idea came to mind. I sent Jade a text and told her that I'd wait on her if she wanted to stop by for dinner. While I waited for her response, I made myself a promise that I'd be at the gym every night that week working off such a late dinner if she accepted. She did.

She arrived at nine thirty with a bottle of red wine tucked under her arm. She held it up when I opened the door. "I figure since we're blowing our diet, we should do it right. Besides, red wine is healthy now and then." She opened the bottle and poured the wine while I put the steaks on the grill. We sat outside on my tiny patio and enjoyed the evening. "Have you been drunk since your accident?" she asked.

I thought for a minute. "I had a drink at Miranda's one night. That's as close as I've come. Are you worried?"

"No. I just wondered what effect it had on you."

"Well, if I keep drinking on an empty stomach, we'll find out. A friend of mine is a cop. I can get her to drop off a pair of cuffs to keep me in line."

She smiled and shook her head. "You don't have to do that."

A moment of silence went by. "I have a pair in my truck anyway." My eyes bugged, and Jade threw back her head and laughed. "You're so easy."

"You're as bad as Miranda. I'm taking the kid gloves off with you." I stood and flipped the steaks, then reclaimed my seat beside her. "What TV shows do you like? Or do you ever have time to watch any?"

"I don't have a TV. If I did, I'd never have a chance to turn it on."

"How do you spend your spare time?"

Jade stretched her long legs. "I read a lot. History fascinates me, and I enjoy mysteries and intrigue."

"Mom, or Momma Donahue rather, was a big-time reader. I got my first library card with her. She took Miranda and me smelling like two wet dogs because we had been building a tree house. I still remember picking out my first book and the way it smelled just like the library."

"You never did that with your real mom?" Jade asked tentatively.

"No, she was always working to take care of my brother and me as a single parent. Saturday nights were ours, though. She'd take us to the movies. We'd sneak in snacks because we couldn't afford to buy them at the theater." I was silent for a moment as I thought about her. Those movie nights were just about all I could remember. "My brother always balked because he had to watch kid movies, he's older than me."

"What happened to him?"

"We just drifted apart. He was in the military for a long time, then he just wandered." I shook my head. "I have no idea what he does for a living. Sometimes, he just shows up. That's how I got the car. He bought it on the spur of the moment and realized he couldn't afford it, even though it was used. I took over his note, and he left on the bus never saying where he was going." I looked at Jade. "Do you have siblings?"

"No, I was an only child."

"Must've been hard on you losing your parents," I said, hoping I wouldn't upset her.

She stared at her feet for a long time. "It was, and one day, maybe I'll tell you about it."

I took that as my cue to stay clear of that topic until she was ready. "How's Guy?"

She tossed her head to the side to move the hair from her eyes. "He's discovered the springy door stops on the baseboards. Last night around three, he played me a tune."

"How very creative and kind of him to share his music."

"I told him the same thing, though not in those words, and I punctuated with a pillow. I awoke to it again at five, and we had coffee," she said with a smile.

"He takes it with a lot of cream, I presume."

"No, black. I got out of the shower and found him with his face in my cup."

I laughed while I summoned my courage. "Marty has been talking to our friend Deb. She's the one I told you about who tossed us out of her house. She's agreed to have dinner with us tomorrow night at Miranda's. We're getting together around eight. Would you like to come with me if you can get off early?" I started rambling, certain that she would say no. "It's nothing special, just burgers. If you can't, I understand. I don't wanna cause you problems on your—"

"You ramble when you're nervous."

"Sorry."

"Yes."

I narrowed my eyes. "You're agreeing that I'm sorry, or are you saying you'll go?"

With a straight face, she said, "You'll figure it out tomorrow night at seven forty-five."

I grinned as I got up to check the steaks.

"Are you sure this is okay?" Jade stretched her legs out and rested her feet on the coffee table, mimicking my pose.

I finished chewing a piece of steak and nodded. "Don't you put your feet on yours?"

"Don't have one. No TV, no point."

"Speaking of," I picked up the remote, "wanna watch?"

She shook her head and smiled. "No, I want you to tell me about your friends."

I tossed the remote on the couch. "Well, there's Miranda and her partner, Marty. Deb's girlfriend is Angel, then there's Lonna and Paige, but they won't be there tomorrow night. We're planning a party reception thing for them because they recently sneaked off and got married."

Jade stabbed at her salad. "I'm looking forward to meeting them. They probably have stories to tell."

"And they'll all be before my accident. I'm not that woman anymore, so consider that when they start yapping because they will at the slightest provocation."

"I think it'd be interesting to hear about the old Sloan. Will there be pictures?" she asked with an evil grin.

"Oh, please, don't go there. Miranda has stacks of albums. It's not a pretty sight." I shivered at the thought.

Jade took a sip of her wine. "You have nothing to worry about. I like the new Sloan. I can't imagine anything they might say or show me will change that."

I felt a flush rise up from my neck. Her words thrilled me. I continued eating with a smile.

Once the dishes were put away, Jade got ready to leave. I wanted so much to ask her to stay. Just sleeping next to her, not even touching, would've been a dream. When we were apart, I thought about her endlessly, and when we were together, I didn't want it to end.

"Thank you for dinner." She was standing by the door looking awkward, and I was fairly certain like me she didn't know how to bring our evening to a close.

"Can I hug you?" I asked.

She tilted her head and smiled. "Can you?"

"I promise to pull away if I can't control myself." That statement had dual connotations because once I had her in my arms, I wasn't sure I could let go.

She grinned for a second, then her expression turned serious. "I trust you." She swallowed, and her voice sounded raspy. "I haven't been able to say that to many people." She opened her arms, and I rushed in.

Her body molded perfectly with mine and felt so warm and soft. I closed my eyes and pushed all thought from my mind and dwelled on what I was feeling.

"What are my emotions telling you?" she asked nervously.

"That's a daring question for someone in your shoes. I don't know if I would have the courage to ask if the roles were reversed." I wrapped my arms tighter around her waist. "You feel...joy, warmth...like you belong right here." I wanted to cry because that was exactly what I felt.

"Do you feel the same?" She pushed me back gently and looked me in the eye. I couldn't speak, and I knew she saw the tears forming. I nodded. She pulled me back in and held me for a moment. I felt her reluctance to let me go. "I'm looking forward to tomorrow night," she said as she backed away and opened the door.

I watched her go with a sad smile. I thought I understood then what Miranda was saying about the precipice. I was on the edge, and I knew she was, too. And in that moment, I accepted that I had been given an extraordinary gift...in more ways than one.

Chapter 16

At seven fifty, Jade walked out of the gym wearing a deep green T-shirt and a pair of tan cargo shorts. She looked magnificent. The dark green brought out the color in her eyes. I stared at her a minute or two when she got in my car.

"What?" she asked when I didn't immediately drive off.

"You're stunning."

"I was thinking the same about you. Sometimes, I forget to say what I'm thinking. She looked at my shorts and T-shirt. "You look lovely tonight, but do you know when I find you most attractive?"

I shook my head.

She grinned. "When you've just finished working out and your hair is a mess and sticking to your face. It gets really wavy, and your face is flushed..." Her voice trailed off as she looked away. "It's sexy."

"*So* we'll be running the air tonight," I said as I switched it on and rolled up the windows. "You've managed to raise the heat index in the car by a hundred degrees."

I left the parking lot with the sound of Jade's laughter and my heart pounding a delightful beat.

Deb and Angel weren't due to arrive until eight thirty, and as planned, Jade and I arrived early, so we could discuss, as Marty said, "what not to say to Deb." Marty and Jade seemed to hit it off the minute they met, but then again, Marty had that effect on people. She was so open and friendly that everyone fell under her charm, and Jade was no exception.

We gathered in the living room, and after some small talk, Miranda got down to business. "Sloan, Marty and I have been talking about something, and we'd like your take on it." She looked over at Jade. "I'm sorry that your first visit with us might be a tense one. Sloan said she's told you about the situation with Deb. We're not gossiping about her. We're worried, and we're trying to help."

Jade nodded. "I understand."

Miranda looked back at me. "Marty and I think you should touch Angel. I think it's the best way to find out what she knows without offending her and making a difficult situation worse."

I wasn't prepared for the request. "I don't know." I looked at Jade and wondered what was going through her head.

"Sloan, this is a gift," Miranda said. "I know you don't feel that way, but you can use this to help someone we care a lot about. We don't want to know what you see, but if you can figure out Angel's feelings on this, we'll know if we have an ally or not."

"Deb's fiercely protective about her situation," Marty said. "She won't even come close to discussing it. We're at an impasse, and I don't know what else to do."

We never had a chance to discuss it further. There was a knock on the door, then we heard Deb's voice. "Hello, we're here."

Marty stood and greeted them warmly with hugs. Deb's gaze moved to Miranda, and I watched them stare at each other before moving in for a big hug. It appeared that Deb had forgiven. Jade and I stood, and I moved around the coffee table, hoping to put a barrier between Deb and me. I introduced her to Jade, and Deb gave her a quick hug. Deb made a move toward me. I knew she was going to hug me, and I made a split-second decision.

Through her eyes, I saw her dressing and how she layered on clothes to hide weight loss that was even more profound than the last time I'd peeked into her mind. She hoped that we wouldn't notice. She hoped that dinner wasn't heavy. She hoped that Angel wouldn't hear her in the downstairs bathroom after dinner as she pulled on another shirt.

When she released me, I smiled and backed away. I turned and took two purposeful steps toward Angel, and I hugged her tightly. She was lying on her side, holding Deb as she slept. She could feel the sharpness of Deb's hip bone beneath her fingertips. The feel of it sickened me. It had been ages since they'd made love, Angel thought. She sighed softly as she wondered what to do about Deb's secretive ways. What could she say? Could their relationship withstand her betrayal of confiding in another?

I feigned a coughing fit and slipped into the bathroom to compose myself when Angel released me. I looked at myself in the mirror and wondered how I could possess such information and not do something about it. I just didn't know what that something should be.

"Are you all right?" Jade asked softly when I walked back into the room.

Miranda had Deb and Angel in the kitchen fixing drinks. Jade and Marty stared at me with worried expressions. I shook my head. "No, I'm not. It's not good."

Marty put a hand to her chest and exhaled loudly before joining the others in the kitchen.

Jade walked over and stood directly in front of me, blocking the view of the others if they returned. "You need to go back in the bathroom and wash your face with cool water. It's very flushed. She reached out slowly, giving me time to prepare for her touch and stroked my cheek. "While you're in there, take a few deep breaths and let them out slowly. Try to push the thoughts from your mind because it's very obvious that you're upset."

"Come with me."

Jade looked over her shoulder. "To the bathroom?"

"If I'm still flushed when we come out, they'll think we were kissing or something. They'll tease me, but Deb and Angel won't suspect something's wrong." I turned and Jade followed behind me. When she closed the door, I sagged against the counter and folded my arms across my chest. "Jade, I can't tell you what I saw, but it's worse."

Jade's face showed compassion as she reached up slowly and stroked my hair. "Sometimes we have to hide our emotions. Put this in a box and shove it into the back of your mind for later. For tonight, recall a happy thought and focus on that." A slight smile moved across her face. "If it were me, I'd dwell on our day on the coast."

I couldn't help but smile then.

"Where do they keep the washcloths?"

I pointed to the cabinet behind her. Jade opened it and took one out. She ran water over it and wringed it out before holding it to my cheek. "It's just like acting, Sloan. Go out there and play your part."

She moved the cloth to my other cheek, and I wondered how many times she'd coached herself that way and why.

We did take some ribbing when we joined the others, and Jade played it up, taking the pressure off me. "We…um…will pay for the damages to your bathroom. I hope you have two. If not, everyone might want to consider the gas station down the street." She looked at me with a mischievous smile. "I had no idea you were that acrobatic."

"Oh," Angel pointed at Jade, "she's going to fit in perfectly with this group. You better hang on to her, Sloan."

I winked at Jade. "I plan to."

Over dinner, we discussed the plans for the party. We'd have it at Marty and Miranda's since their place was the biggest. Deb volunteered to send the invitations and supply half the liquor. Miranda, Marty, and I would take care of the food and decorations. We picked a date according to Lonna's work schedule, and our surprise was planned.

"So, Jade, how'd you and Sloan meet?" Angel asked as if she didn't already know.

"I'm a personal trainer at the gym. Sloan and Miranda aren't my clients, but I try to help whip them into shape anyway."

"Whip is right," Miranda said with a groan. "She developed an exercise plan for us that's a killer. Don't get me started on the diet."

"Well, Sloan looks no worse for wear," Deb said with a smile. "She must be into pain."

"It's not as bad as Miranda makes it sound. She's just a weenie."

Miranda wadded up her napkin and threw it at me. "All right, Ms. Leg Cramp, keep it up."

"Oh, I get those a lot," Deb said. "Especially when I run, they're excruciating."

"Hydration and nutrition are key to avoiding those. Protein is essential for someone who is working out or doing strenuous labor," Jade said. "I tell my clients to drink at least sixteen ounces of water and a low sugar sports drink before they come in for a workout." Jade draped her arm over the back of my chair. "I can tell who is following the diet plan by the way they perform. If they're face down on the mat in the first ten minutes, I know they're not fueling their bodies."

"What's on the diet plan?" Deb asked.

"Low sugar because it hypes you up for a short time but doesn't provide fuel that muscle needs. Chicken and fish are the main meats, but the plan does allow red in moderation. You can have all the beans you want, but that tends to cause some embarrassment for some," she said with a grin. "Spinach and broccoli are good, too, all of which makes you gaseous, hence the embarrassment."

I looked at Miranda and laughed. Aside from cutlery, she had nothing else to throw. Marty moved her fork just in case.

"I'll be happy to share the plan with you if you want," Jade said, looking at Deb.

"I'd really appreciate that." Deb flashed a look at Miranda, and I felt the muscles in my stomach tighten.

Marty quickly changed the subject. "Has anyone considered what we're going to get Lonna and Paige as wedding presents? I mean, we can't go with the norm. They're already living together, so housewares are out."

"Sex toys," Miranda and I said in unison and laughed.

"That really is a good idea," Deb said with a grin. "We could have a lot of fun with that."

Marty the methodical turned a fresh page in her notebook. "So who's getting what? We don't all wanna show up with strap-ons."

I flushed and cast a sideways glance at Jade. She was smiling back at me, seemingly enjoying my embarrassment.

"Oh! I call the strap-on," Deb said. She looked at Angel. "You can handle the dildo, can't you, baby?"

A chorus of "ohs" went around the table as one of Angel's dark eyebrows rose.

Marty pointed at Deb with her pen. "You are so sleeping on the couch tonight!"

"I saw a sexy cop uniform the other day. Really kinky," Miranda said. "I call that."

"And where exactly did you see such a thing?" Marty asked, looking at her.

Miranda shrugged nonchalantly. "At Sloan's store."

Everyone looked at me, including Jade. I raised my hands. "She's full of shit."

"Actually, I saw it in a magazine at the station." Miranda winked at me. "And what will you be bringing?"

"I dunno."

Everyone at the table guffawed. "Don't sit there in front of your new girlfriend and act all puritanical," Deb said with a laugh. "We all know your reputation."

"Expand on that please," Jade said with a smile.

"I'll bring vibrators and lubes," I said loudly before anyone could comment. "And that draws this conversation to a close."

"Do you mind driving" I asked Jade as we walked out to the car.

"Can I squeal the tires?" She took the keys and batted her eyes.

"Not in the neighborhood, but you can burn off all the rubber you want when we get on the highway."

We were jovial until we were in the privacy of my car. I sank low in the seat and sighed.

"You did great, Sloan. I'm very proud of you for handling it so well."

I ran both hands through my hair. "This is a big problem with Deb, and I have no idea where to start."

"You're right," Jade said. "I have no idea what you saw tonight, but I did see the effect it had on you. I'd suggest you and Miranda visit a therapist that specializes in eating disorders." Jade glanced at me. "If you can get Angel to go with you, that'd be better. Let a professional tell you what your next step should be."

"All right, I'll talk to Miranda about that tomorrow. We'll come up with a plan to talk to Angel, and if she won't go with us, we'll do it on our own."

Jade came to the main highway and stopped. "Are you tired?"

"No, but I don't have to get up as early as you do."

Instead of making a right, which would've taken us home, she went left. "I have something I want to show you. Since you've lived here all your life, you've probably already been there."

I had no idea where she was taking me, but I was willing to go.

"Like I said, I haven't done a lot of exploring, but I did find this place one night when I had a lot on my mind." She turned off the highway and I grinned.

"I know exactly where you're taking me." The road ended at the bay in a small parking area a couple of yards from the water. There were no lights, but I could hear the waves lapping gently at the shore when she killed the engine.

Jade inhaled deeply, then let out a contented sigh. "Just listen to that."

"Let's get out and sit on the hood. It's a clear night, maybe we'll luck out and see a shooting star." Jade was a bit hesitant to get on my car, but when I climbed up and leaned my back against the windshield, she did the same albeit more carefully. The heat of the engine warmed my legs, making me feel like I was in a cozy nest. When Jade settled next to me, I felt my cares drift away on the breeze. Overhead, the night sky was filled with what looked like a billion stars. I tucked my hands behind my head and decided to bask in the moment. "This was a brilliant idea."

"I'm glad you didn't mind coming." Jade seemed to be as content as I was.

"Tell me something about you. Anything." I looked over at her.

She was thoughtful for a moment. "When I was a little girl, we moved to a house in the country, and there was a field next door full of wildflowers about waist high. I used to walk through it and pretend it was the ocean. I'd get down on my knees and imagine that I was looking at beds of coral like the ones I'd seen on TV." She laughed. "A child's imagination is limitless. I think now, if I walked through that field, all I would think about were the bugs and the itchiness of the weeds. I probably wouldn't go into it at all." She looked at me. "Your turn. Tell me about a childhood memory."

"I made the coolest clubhouse out of a wisteria bush. There was no telling how old that thing was. They're really vines, but this had never been tended and sat out in the middle of the yard with nothing to climb, so it wound around itself. I took a piece of plywood and tossed it in the middle of the bush. Then I climbed up on it, and as long as I stayed down, I was completely hidden. It was my secret spot until I spotted Colin trying to whittle something out of a piece of wood. I climbed down unseen and gathered a handful of rocks. I hit him like four times before he spotted me."

Jade laughed. "How old were you?"

"Probably around seven. He wasn't allowed to have a pocket knife until he was fifteen, and he'd managed to trade his binoculars for one. I threatened to tell if he didn't leave me alone. Apparently, my threat had little effect. He wanted to beat my ass, but he was too big to crawl through the vines. I ended up staying there half of the afternoon until Mom called us for dinner."

"You were mischievous then?"

"Very, though most of it was directed at my brother. Poor boy, no wonder he doesn't keep in touch much. After I met Miranda, I had a new target, but she was as bad as I was. I learned early on that she was far more skilled. I bet you weren't, though. You were probably an angelic child."

Jade's sigh was carried off in the breeze. "I'm sure I had my moments, but that seems like ancient history."

"You're not that old."

"You're trying to get me to admit how old I am, aren't you?" Jade chuckled but said nothing else.

"Wanna hear me sing? It's really bad. Dogs usually howl when they hear it, and birds drop from the sky. I bet I don't even get through the first verse of the country song I wrote before you're screaming out your age."

"Thirty-six. I'll take your word for it. And you're still mischievous."

A cool breeze blew in off the water, and I shivered. "Are you cold?"

"Yeah, it's getting a bit nippy and probably late. Are you ready?" She laid my keys on my thigh.

"I know we have to go," I said regretfully. I hopped down and was surprised to hear Jade behind me as her shoes shuffled over the asphalt.

I was about to turn and ask if she wanted to drive when I heard her say, "I want to kiss you."

I turned slowly. All I could make out was her figure in the darkness. "Did you just say you wanted—"

"To kiss you, yes."

My heart started to pound. "I hate to take the romance and spontaneity out of this moment, but," I opened the car door and moved behind it, "I don't know what full body contact and a kiss would do to me. I mean, I would love that, but I don't want to mess up...I probably wouldn't be able to think about anything else but what that feels like because I've wanted for so long to—"

"You really do ramble when you're nervous." Jade moved closer and put her hands on the door frame.

"I'm sorry, I can't help it. I've dreamed about this moment since the day you touched my hand and gave me hope that I might be able to experience...more." I shivered again, but this time, it wasn't caused by the cool evening breeze.

Very slowly, she reached over and stroked the back of my hand. "Don't apologize. It means you care. I should've admitted this before." She licked her lips. "I like that we have to take it slow. I think too often people end up in bed together, then later realize all they have between them is the physical attraction."

I swallowed hard. "I'd still like that kiss. Can you give me a second to just…close my eyes and focus?"

"Yeah, I'll give you a couple."

I closed my eyes and concentrated on the pounding in my ears. My heart was racing in anticipation, then I felt the lightest touch against my lips. She pulled away slightly and met me again. I wanted to feel her body press into mine, but there was something so sensual about that kiss. The only thing I could physically feel besides the door that I had a death grip on was the softness of her lips, the caress of her tongue. The sweetest kiss I had ever received was also the hottest, and it burned through me like fire.

"Slow is a good thing, right?" I said with a nervous laugh when she pulled away. Her emotions echoed through my mind—joy, excitement, desire.

"I thought so until a moment ago." Jade took two awkward steps back, tripping over her own feet. She disappeared into the darkness, then I heard the passenger door open. I climbed into the car and looked at her. Jade's expression was one part bewilderment and the other slight amusement. My gaze trailed down to the flush creeping up her neck and along her jaw. "Wow" was all she said.

"Yeah."

I pushed the Mustang to her limits on the way back to the gym. Jade grabbed a hold of the door handle and looked at me. "Are you in a hurry?"

"Yes, because when we get to the gym, I'm gonna kiss you again."

Chapter 17

The next morning when my alarm clock went off, I awoke with a smile. I pressed my fingers to my lips, reveling in the memories of Jade's kisses.

With the center console of my car acting as a barrier between us, I filled my hands with her hair and pulled her as close as I could. Both of us were breathing heavily like two teenagers who had never had a moment alone as we made out. I wasn't sure how much time had passed as we steamed up the windows. My heart ached with a sweet loneliness that I'd never experienced as I watched her climb into that old truck. My lips felt bruised and chapped as I ran my fingers over them. "So this is what it's like to be totally smitten," I said aloud in the darkness.

Miranda walked into the store around ten in her uniform with a radio squawking on her hip. Her expression was dour as she said "good morning." The events of the previous evening pushed away my giddiness like a bulldozer.

"Marty said you looked like shit after you touched Deb and Angel." Miranda leaned on the counter and looked at me with dread.

"Our talk didn't have any effect on Deb. She's more intent on hiding her weight loss. She still thinks she needs to lose a few more pounds. I think Angel might be open to talk to us if we approach her gently."

"And then what?" Miranda asked wearily. "Some sort of intervention where we all gang up on her? Deb's not the type of person to be affected by that. She'll throw us all out, including Angel."

"Jade suggested we see a therapist that specializes in eating disorders. Maybe he or she can tell us what to do next."

Miranda rubbed the bridge of her nose as she considered what I'd said. "I can talk to some of the docs at the hospital. I'm sure they can recommend someone."

"Do you think Marty would be willing to talk to Angel? She's got that gentle way about her, and Angel might be more receptive."

Miranda nodded. "Good plan. I'll talk to her about it."

I poked her in the arm. "Don't look so worried. At least we've gone from scratching our heads to a plan."

Miranda smiled slightly. "Jade held her own with the gang pretty well last night."

"Yeah, she did." I felt my face flush and watched as Miranda's brow rose. "She kissed me."

"No shit?" Miranda's face transformed into a full-on smile.

"It was one of the greatest feelings." I shook my head to dispel the dreaminess that washed over me. "I've never felt this way about anyone. I wonder what she's doing when we're apart, and I find myself coming up with ways to see her all the time. She's just so…different."

"Actually," Miranda looked at me seriously, "you're the one who's different. You've changed and opened yourself up to something more than a casual fling. I'm so happy for you."

"Couldn't have come this far without you. Thank you."

Miranda grinned. "I still get to live vicariously through you, though this time it won't be through your exploits, just your happiness."

"You're already happy. I might just get to experience what you have now."

A shrill tone emanating from the radio on Miranda's hip made us both jump. "I gotta go. Have fun at the health club tonight. We both know you're going without me."

At six, I closed the store. I changed into my workout clothes and ate a piece of chicken for fuel. I couldn't wait to see Jade. Even if we did nothing but stare across the room at each other, I was thrilled. Just to be in her presence made me happy. But that giddiness evaporated when I walked in and saw Jacquelyn.

I hadn't noticed that she'd not been around. Her presence was like a vacuum sucking all the joy from the room as I stretched. She was barely sweating. Jade stood with her arms folded as Jacquelyn halfheartedly worked with the free weights. Unlike the rest of Jade's clients who worked silently or released an occasional groan, Jacquelyn yammered constantly. I caught bits and pieces of what she was saying, and although she claimed she'd been on a business trip, it sounded more like she spent her time in bars.

Jade looked up in the mirror and caught my eye. She nodded, and I caught just the hint of a smile.

"So anyway," Jacquelyn said loudly, calling Jade's attention back to her. "I won't be traveling again for a while. Maybe—" Her voice lowered again, and I could see Jade shaking her head and the perturbed look that crossed Jacquelyn's face.

I felt hostility rise up in me again. The temptation to leave and rid myself of that woman's presence was strong, but I wasn't going to let Jade suffer alone. I was sure that's exactly what Jacquelyn would've preferred, so I mentally talked myself down. *Look at Jade's body language. She's totally closed off. Notice the expression on her face. She doesn't look at you like that. And last night, it was you she was kissing and panting over.* I smiled then, cocky and confident, and no one noticed.

When Jacquelyn's time was up, she sauntered off, watching Jade in the mirror. Jade was watching me and my heart soared. She instructed her next client to begin her stretches before making her way over.

"I was thinking," I said with a smile, "the weather is supposed to be great this weekend. We could pack a lunch and head out to St. George. I'll bring a wheelbarrow."

"I was thinking along the same lines," Jade said as she watched her client. "We could spend the whole day on the beach, and I could cook for you that evening. How about Sunday?" I wanted Saturday *and* Sunday. She looked at me then as if reading my mind. "I have to work Saturday. By the time I get out of here, most of the day will be gone."

"You'll probably be hungry after a long day like that. I could cook and you could relax."

Jade smiled then and not her usual gym smile. "I should be done here around three."

"Then it's a date. Now go to work before the temptation to kiss you overwhelms me and I embarrass us both."

Jade hesitated a second and grinned before walking away.

I finished my workout and stood in the corner with a bottle of water to cool down and watch Jade. She was suspended on two parallel bars and was pulling her knees up as she demonstrated for her client. The muscles in Jade's arms and abdomen flexed as she lifted her legs. She was talking the entire time without any strain in her voice. I was mesmerized. My mind wandered over the planes of her stomach and chest and wondered what it would feel like to kiss that soft skin and feel the rigidity of the muscle against my lips.

"Where are you?" Jade asked softly.

I jumped when I realized she was standing beside me. "I was just...wondering when I'd be able to do that thing with the parallel bars as effortlessly as you do."

Jade cocked her head to the side. "Mm-hmm, I know what a woman in lust looks like."

"I bet you do," I said, meeting her gaze.

"The question is, do you?" She grinned. "I think not, or you would've already seen it in my eyes." She walked away and looked over her shoulder with a wink.

The weekend could not get here fast enough.

Miranda was at my door the next morning when I opened for business. She held a bag that contained two yogurts and a bottle of apple juice for me orange for her. "Go to the gym last night?" she asked as she walked in.

"Yep, got a date for the weekend." I had a skip in my step as I went back to the counter, eager to work on my next creation, a shell necklace for Jade.

Miranda took a stool and opened her yogurt. "When you say the weekend, do you mean one night or the whole enchilada?"

"She has to work Saturday, but we're having dinner that night, then Sunday, we're gonna spend the day at St. George Island." I threaded a shell onto a piece of deep green cord and began to weave the braid. "I can't wait."

"So…you've kissed. This weekend could lead to…"

I looked up slowly from my creation. "I have no expectations. Whatever happens will happen on its own time."

"Are you ready for that?" Miranda asked before popping a spoonful of yogurt into her mouth.

"Oh, I'm ready," I said with a growl that made us both laugh.

"You know what I mean."

I went back to work on the necklace. "When we kissed, I couldn't focus on anything but what I was feeling, it was easy. I can't imagine that I won't be able to control the images if it goes beyond that."

"Sex is a full body contact sport. You're gonna feel every inch of her pressed against you. This will be the biggest test thus far."

I shivered as thoughts of what Miranda described danced through my mind.

"And then there are her emotions." Miranda stopped talking and eating and stared off into space. "What if she has regrets or is unsatisfied?"

Miranda had successfully heated me up, then poured a big fat bucket of ice water over my head without ever having to lift a finger. "Sometimes, it's a real love-hate relationship with you."

She shrugged and went back to eating. "It was just a thought."

"Thanks for sharing. Now I'm going to have real performance anxiety. Probably won't be able to relax to save my life."

"She's a great kisser, I bet." Miranda waved her spoon.

I was not going on that roller coaster ride again. "Shut up."

Miranda chuckled. "So she must really love the beach like you do, or else she doesn't give a rat's ass and will go anywhere to be with you."

"I hope it's both."

"Oh! Talked to a doc at the hospital, and she gave me the name of someone to call. She's a nutritionist, and she'll be able to recommend a good therapist. Marty's gonna talk to Angel today and see if she'll be willing to see her with us."

"Excellent, but be prepared for just me and you going if Angel chickens out. She's afraid of irreparably damaging her relationship with Deb. She might not want to get into the driver's seat on this one."

"That's just weird to me. If it were Marty, I'd do whatever I had to get her well."

"You and Marty have a different relationship. Deb's got a lot of insecurities, she's defensive about everything. I imagine Angel has to walk on a lot of eggshells with her."

"She's definitely defensive about her weight loss regimen. Did you see how she sneered at me the other night when she and Jade were talking about the diet plan? I had to bite my lip. I felt like she was daring me to say something."

The mention of Jade's name made me smile, and my thoughts went to her. I wondered what she was doing and if she'd really like the necklace I was making her.

"You're not even in the room with me right now, are you?"

I looked at Miranda. "Sorry, faded out there for a second."

"Yeah," Miranda said with a chuckle, "skipping through Jade wonderland, no doubt."

"That beach house you rented for your anniversary last year, was it expensive?"

"Oh, you little minx," Miranda said with a chuckle. "They rent by the week. Are you going to close your store for that long?" Miranda tossed her empty yogurt container in the trash. "I could work for you on my days off, and Kaylie could take the weekend."

"Thanks, that's really sweet of you," I said with a smile. "It's only twenty minutes away. I could still come in to work. Jade probably isn't going to be able to get off for that amount of time anyway. We could spend our evenings and a weekend there, though."

"Business is slow for them right now. I've been getting a lot of emails with special rates. I'm sure they'd give you a good deal if I call." Miranda cleared her throat. "That's an overnight sleepover," she said seriously. "Are you ready for that?"

"It has two bedrooms, right?"

Miranda snorted. "Do you really think you'll go to your own corners when it's bedtime?"

"We might," I said as I felt my face heat. "She said she's happy we're taking it slow." I shook my head. "I just want to be with her. It doesn't have to be anything more than that."

Miranda gave me that warm googly smile she used when she thought something was sweet. "Move over and let me use your computer."

Chapter 18

Jade looked beat when she showed up at my house Saturday afternoon. It was just after three thirty when she arrived and dinner wasn't going to be ready until six. So I talked her into lying on my couch and watching a movie. We were halfway into *Castaway* when I glanced over and noticed she was asleep.

I watched her chest rise and fall in a steady rhythm. Her hands lay across her stomach and twitched slightly as she descended deeper into sleep. My eyes enjoyed a little feast as my gaze moved over long, well-defined legs. I'd never noticed the pale line just above her right knee, a two-inch scar from an injury that looked like it hadn't healed well.

I studied her hands next. I couldn't imagine those long fingers typing away on a keyboard. Jade was all strength and physicality. I couldn't see her at a desk job or anything that required her to be complacent for long periods of time. The skin of her arms looked soft, but I knew if I ran my fingers over it, I would feel the firm muscle beneath even in relaxation. I had avoided her face, saving it like I would when I ate a piece of cake up to that last icing-filled corner. Her lips were slightly parted, and I smiled as I remembered how they'd felt against mine—warm, full, and incredibly soft. Her face serene in slumber was absolutely gorgeous.

But as I sat there looking at her, I realized what made Jade so beautiful. Behind the aloof exterior that she was allowing me to gradually see past was a sincerely lovely soul. I'd seen into her mind and felt her emotions, and with all the hurts of her past, there was no hint of bitterness or malice. Just desire to be loved and cherished and with equal intensity a longing to return that love and adoration.

In her search, she'd chosen the wrong people, and for a second, I wondered why she'd chosen me. Was she trying to break the pattern or was she subconsciously drawn to what I used to be? Regardless, I was determined to be everything she wanted because as I sat there looking at her, I felt my heart slip away.

"How long was I out?" Jade walked into the kitchen behind me.

I turned from the salad I was making and grinned at her standing there with her hair pointing in all directions. "Almost two hours. You must've needed it, though, because my couch isn't that comfortable."

"I'm so sorry." Jade scrubbed at her face.

"Don't be. It made me happy to know that you feel that comfortable here."

"Can I help with anything? I can finish slicing that tomato if you want."

I shook my head. "Nope, I've already grilled the tilapia and veggies."

"I can fix drinks." Jade reached past me and pulled two glasses out of the cabinet. "What would you like?"

"Tea, no ice."

"No ice?" Jade opened the fridge and pulled out the pitcher.

"It's cold enough. Ice just melts and spoils the taste."

"Is this unsweetened?" Jade asked as she poured the tea.

"Um…no."

"Ha! You sugar junkie." Jade wagged a finger at me. "I bet if I looked in your pantry, there'd be sweets." She took a sip from my glass and screwed up her face. "Oh, God, there's enough sugar in here to send me into orbit." She set the glass down and headed for the pantry.

I dropped the knife and made it around the counter to block her. "It's not safe. Don't go in there."

"What's gonna get me—the Pillsbury Doughboy?" Jade grinned.

"Him and the Keebler Elves. Stay back for your own good."

Jade's eyes went round. "Sloan!"

I held up a finger. "Now look, those cookies have been in there since before I went on the diet. I haven't thrown them out in case of emergency. I'm losing inches. I can wear shorts I haven't been able to get into for years."

"Oh, really?" Jade said in a challenging tone. "Lift your shirt. Let me see your belly."

Unlike Jade and the other women at the gym, I did not work out wearing only a sports bra and shorts, so she wasn't going to be able to see my improvements.

"Show me the belly." Jade inched closer with a grin.

"It was pudgy when I first started working out, but it's improved, I can assure you." I took a step back as she moved closer.

"So let me see it."

I took another step back. "Um, no." I turned and ran.

Jade chased me into the living room laughing. I stood on one side of the couch and she on the other. "Are you hiding an ugly tattoo?" she teased as she rocked back and forth, making me do the same.

"Nope, no tattoos."

"Is your belly button an outie?" Jade darted to one end of the couch while I ran to the other.

"Nope, it's an innie, and it's impeccably clean." I couldn't help but giggle.

Jade backed up, forcing me to move in front of the couch again. Her eyes twinkled with mischief as she watched me contemplate my escape.

"The fish is going to burn."

Jade put her hands on her hips. "You are such a bad liar. You already told me you took the fish and the veggies off."

"Oh, yeah, right."

"Is it hairy? Is that why you're hiding it?" she asked, making a face.

"It is not," I said indignantly. "It's pale, though. I haven't sunned it yet." Jade was over the back of the couch in a flash, the coffee table was only a light skip to her after that. She caught me by the tail end of my shirt before I could get away. "All right," I said with a laugh, "here it is." I turned and lifted my shirt up until it fell just below my bra.

Jade was grinning from ear to ear as she looked it over. She reached out a hand. "May I touch?"

"Yes, but be careful of the muscle, it's razor sharp. I felt the muscles I really did have quiver beneath her touch. She ran her hands down the center of my stomach. Her feelings came fast. She was pleased with the hardness she felt, which quickly gave way to an arousal that matched mine. And then she stepped back.

"You really have been working hard," she said in the professional tone she used at the gym.

"Do you need to check the rest of me?" I asked, emboldened by the fire she'd stoked.

Jade looked taken aback for a split second, then smiled. "Yes, I eventually will."

"I hope I measure up," I said over my shoulder as I walked back into the kitchen.

I heard her mumble something and exhale loudly.

We were grinning like two schoolgirls with a secret when we sat to eat. "This is delicious," Jade said after her first bite of fish. "I hope I measure up when I cook for you," she said with a wink.

"I have no doubts in your abilities," I said cockily. Jade averted her gaze as her face flushed. "I've been pondering something, and I'd like to know if you'd be interested."

She looked at me expectantly as she wiped her mouth with her napkin.

"Miranda rented a beach house on Alligator Point last year. She thinks she can get the owners to give me a good deal on it." My heart melted when I saw the excitement on Jade's face. "We could get it for a week and still be able to work during the day. It's only a twenty-minute drive. But we could spend our nights and a weekend—"

"Whatever the cost is, I'll pay it."

"I'll take that as a yes then?" I said with a laugh.

"Yes, yes, yes. I can make the reservation or I can give you my credit card." Jade was practically bouncing up and down in her seat.

"It's my treat." I took a bite of the fish and realized that my excitement had trumped my appetite.

Jade shook her head and put her fork down. "We go everywhere in your car and you've fed me for a while now. This will be my treat."

"I buy the groceries then. Deal?"

Jade narrowed her eyes. "I'll think about that. How soon can we make the reservation?"

"I can call Miranda after dinner if you want."

"Yes." Jade nodded and went back to eating quickly.

By the end of the evening, we'd made reservations for the following week. We'd check in at the beach house at three o'clock Saturday, and it would be ours. We were giddy and excited as we planned what we'd bring and the meals we'd cook.

"I hate to have to leave you," Jade said when it began to get late. "If we want to get an early start tomorrow, I should probably go."

"I'm so glad you gave me a second chance."

She smiled as she stood and held her hand out. I took it, and she pulled me up from the couch effortlessly. "And I'm so glad you didn't give up."

She was happy. I could feel her joy flowing through me as we walked to the door. "So I'll come by your place and pick you up around seven?" I said, confirming the plan as she stood leaning against the front door.

"I wrote my address down. It's next to your computer. If you have any problems finding me, just call." She squeezed my hand. "Do I need to keep distance between us to kiss you good night?"

"I think I'll be pretty focused on what I'm feeling," I said with a smile.

Jade pulled me against her until our bodies fit snug. A tiny sigh escaped me as she stared into my eyes before lowering her lips to mine. The kiss began tender and sweet, but as her desire met with mine, it coalesced into a white hot heat that started in the pit of my stomach and spread over me like wildfire. Jade moaned as I fisted my hands in her hair and pushed her harder against the door. I stopped short of grinding my hips into hers.

She groaned loudly as I pulled away from her. "I never knew torment could be so sweet." She blinked a couple of times as she looked at me. "Are you okay? Was it too much?"

"I'm not okay." Jade's face fell as the words slipped out of my mouth. "I didn't see anything, that's not it. I just meant to say that your kisses turn me inside out."

Jade's look of concern turned into a wide smile. "Kissing you has the same effect on me. I'll see you in the morning."

"I look forward to it," I said as she opened the door and walked across the porch with a spring in her step.

I tossed and turned for an hour before I got up and poured myself a glass of wine in hopes that it would relax me. Thoughts of Jade filled my mind and mingled with the excitement of the time I would spend with her. When she'd held me in her arms that night, her feelings matched mine—excitement, arousal, joy, and hope.

I couldn't see myself wanting anyone else like I did her. I wanted to be the cause of her laughter. I wanted to hold her when things weren't going well. I wanted…my mind seized upon what was happening to me, though my heart already knew. I had fallen from the precipice—actually, I jumped. Heedless of potential heartbreak with no safety net in sight, I leapt, determined to enjoy the fall.

I heard an alarm going off in the distance. I burrowed deeper into my warm spot, wishing that someone would turn it off, but it kept blaring until I opened one eye. An empty wineglass sat on the coffee table in front of me, and my face was sticking to the leather of the couch. I sat straight up and looked around the room until I realized where I was. A thrill coursed through me as I jumped up and headed for the shower.

I didn't bother drying my hair. Instead, I pulled it through the back of my favorite ball cap and grabbed my things. Kaylie was bright and chipper as I bounded into the store. "Got it all under control, boss. Go enjoy your day."

"Is that a VW Bug I see in the parking lot?"

She nodded with a grin. "It's all mine."

"Congratulations, sweetie," I said as I squeezed her arm. "I have my cell. Call me if you need anything."

"Miranda already called me and said not to bother you even if the store caught on fire. I'm supposed to call her."

"I love that woman!" I laughed as I went back to the house to get one item I'd forgotten, then I was on my way to Jade.

The apartment where she lived was not the ghetto, but it wasn't in one of the nicer areas. She looked a bit nervous as she invited me in and gave me a quick kiss. Guy greeted me the minute I walked in the door and rubbed his body all over my legs until I petted him.

"Would you like some coffee?" Jade asked as she went into the kitchen.

"That'd be great. I didn't have time to make any this morning." I looked around her sparse living room. A daybed she used as a sofa was the only thing in there. Except for the fishnet hanging in the corner, there was nothing on the walls. Her bedroom door was opened, and I peeked in, seeing only a double bed and a table beside it with a lamp. To me, it looked like the home of someone who wanted to be able to pack up and move fast.

The corner with the fishnet was the only thing that indicated the personality of the occupant. There was a small shelf beneath the net where Jade had arranged her shells. I slipped the bag from beneath my arm and pulled out the plaque I'd bought in the store in Apalachicola and placed it on the shelf. I heard Jade gasp when she walked into the room.

"Do you like it?" I asked as she handed me a cup.

"I love it." She looked at me and smiled. "That's what you bought that day and wouldn't admit."

I shrugged. "The odds of me finding anything else with your real name are slim. I couldn't pass it up."

She leaned over and kissed me again. "Thank you." She

sighed and looked around. "My place isn't much. I'm kind of embarrassed of it actually. That's why I asked you to take Guy home with you the day you picked him up."

My first impulse was to make an excuse. To say something like "well, you're not here often," but I wanted to hear what she had to say, so I looked at her expectantly.

"I told you that I move a lot." She held out her hand, indicating for me to take a seat, then joined me on the daybed. "I got into the habit of not collecting a lot of things. It was just easier to pack."

"But you said you liked it here, even thought about putting down a root or two." I tried to keep the panic out of my voice and was disgusted to realize I'd failed.

She took my hand in hers and nodded to the corner where she kept her shells. "That's my first root. Don't look so worried."

I smiled as relief washed over me from her words and the truth I felt in her touch. "Drink your coffee fast. I want to find enough shells today to make two or three roots."

Jade laughed and shook her head. "The shells aren't the root. It's the memory associated with them."

"Aw, that earned you a kiss." I leaned in with the intention of brushing her lips quickly with mine, but that was not to be. We pulled away breathlessly minutes later. "We better make this coffee to go," I said as I stood.

We went old school and had the Beach Boys blaring on the stereo with the windows down. I grinned when we crossed Ochlockonee Bay, and when I glanced at Jade, she was, too. Something about seeing the water made my heart start pumping, and from the expression I noted on Jade's face, she felt the same way.

I pointed to a road at my left. "Alligator Point is down that way, remember?"

"Hey, can we drive down there a sec and see where we're gonna stay?"

I made a U-turn that had the Mustang fishtailing. We were laughing until Jade spotted the bear crossing sign. "They have bears here?"

"Yep, black bears. Every now and then, one will get crazy with the trash diving, and Wildlife Management has to come get it. They release it deeper in the wild. It's not good for them to get too used to people food."

I turned left onto a side street when the road veered to the right and hoped I was going the right way. I'd only looked at the map once, but Miranda had given pretty good directions. "It's gonna be to our right on a road called Trout." We passed Tarpon and Grouper before Jade pointed to the sign we wanted. I turned onto a smaller blacktop. At the end sat the white house with a blue stripe around it sitting high on piers.

"What a cute place." Jade craned her neck, so she could see more of it. "I wish we were staying this week instead of next."

"Me too, but it'll give us something to look forward to while we work."

Jade looked at me then. "I already have something to look forward to every day—you."

"Aw, that earned you another kiss, but you're not going to get it here. I don't wanna be caught making out on this road."

She laughed. "Then hurry up and drive, so I can collect."

I pulled back onto the road, and we looked at the houses along the way. Some were bunched together, but most were spread out. "I'd like to own one of these someday. The water isn't as pretty here because of the river silt, but it's not as commercialized, either. I think what I like most is the solitude."

Jade was thoughtful for a moment. "You could call it Sloan's Solitude."

"I like the sound of that." What I wanted to say is when I got the house, it would be ours, and she could name it whatever she wanted.

St. George Island was a bit more crowded than the first time we visited, so we hiked a good ways until we settled on a private spot. We spread out our blanket and pinned it down with the cooler and our sandals. Jade looked around before pulling off her shirt to reveal a sports bar like the ones she wore at work. She made no move to pull off her board shorts, and I was half glad she wasn't going to parade around in a bikini. I didn't think my heart could take it, and I'd probably pass out or drown in the surf.

I pulled my shirt off and started spraying myself with sun block. Jade lowered her glasses and looked at my bathing suit top. "Does that come with a matching pair of bottoms?"

"It does, but I'll never wear them out in public. I'm too modest and too chunky."

"You're not the least bit chunky. To be honest, I thought you were perfect the first day I saw you at the gym."

"Then why did you put me on that killer exercise program?" I sat beside her.

"You told me in the questionnaire what you wanted your body to look like, so I wrote up a program for you to achieve those results. As a trainer, I think everyone should be fit, but you looked great just the way you were." She held up her hand. "That's not to say you don't look great now."

"Excellent save." I held up my can of SPF 50. "Sunblock?"

"Yes, please." Jade held her hand out for the can, but I did the spraying myself and enjoyed the yelp that accompanied the dance she did when the spray hit her skin. "That was mean," she said, trying to keep a straight face. "There will be paybacks."

I settled down on the blanket. "You deserve it for something. I just can't remember what."

Every sunny day has at least one cloud and ours happened to be two small ones—sunburned, drunk, and obnoxious. Jade and I had been sunning ourselves for about an hour when the two guys passed where we were lying. One whistled, and Jade lifted her head and looked in their direction. The more boisterous of the two grunted and said, "Your momma and poppa must be proud of you. You are one hot bitch."

I sat up and pointed down the beach. "The straight drunk girls are that way." I flopped back down and resumed sunning.

"Prick," Jade said lowly.

"Yep, and that prick is going to be crying for his mommy tomorrow. I don't think I've seen a boiled lobster that shade of red."

Jade looked back at me, nostrils flaring and wide-eyed

with anger. I was getting my first glimpse of her temper, and it seemed to be on the hot side. "What goes through someone's mind to say something like that? Did he think he'd get a favorable response?"

I shaded my eyes with my hand. "He'll probably use that same line again, and some girl as pickled as he is will think it's cute."

She looked back at the two slowly making their way down the beach. "Prick," she said again.

"Want to eat or collect a few shells?" I asked, hoping to chill her out.

"Shells first, food next." Jade stood, then offered me a hand.

I felt rage coursing through her and wondered if she would've pummeled that guy if he would've said more. She certainly wanted to.

"I forgot to pack the wheelbarrow, so go easy." I held up a bag. "I brought lots of these, though."

Jade forced a smile and took a bag. She looked a lot like she did at the gym when her smile was used to express something she really didn't mean. She calmed after we walked a while, then got excited about finding a sand dollar. Her childlike enthusiasm was contagious, and soon my bag was as full as hers. "It's like trick or treating on the beach," I said. "Did you do that when you were a kid?"

"Not really." Jade shook her head. "We always lived out in the country, so going door to door was difficult. My grandmother lived with us until I was twelve, that's when she passed away." Jade's tone was wistful. "She used to take me to the fall festivals. I would eat hot dogs and cotton candy until I was sick."

"I'd love to see pictures of you as a child."

"There aren't any." She averted her gaze. "They were destroyed."

"Was it a house fire or something like that? Is that what happened to your parents?"

Jade thought for a minute as she stared down at the sand. She didn't look at me when she asked, "The things you said you saw in my mind, was that all you saw?"

"I saw a conversation you had with your boss about taking

Jacquelyn as a client, but that's it, other than what I've already told you."

Jade continued to stare at the ground. "I'll tell you about my parents one day. I'm just not ready to talk about it right now, okay?" Her tone wasn't angry or dismissive, just sad.

"I'm sorry I pushed. I was just curious."

"It's okay. Let's go eat."

Jade was normally a voracious eater, but she only picked at her sandwich, and it took her a long time to finish it. We chatted, but at times, she seemed a million miles away, and I regretted asking about her parents and putting a damper on the day. We packed up our things and headed toward the car by late afternoon. She became chatty again when we started talking about the beach house.

"I might be able to extend my weekend if I can talk some of the other trainers into subbing for me. If you took off, would you have to close the store?" Jade asked as we loaded the car.

I debated Miranda's offer to work for me. I could get Kaylie to come in after school, and Miranda said she'd help, too. "I might be able to work something out if you can give me advance warning."

"Okay, I'll talk to them Monday and see what I can come up with."

Jade offered to drive on the way home, and I let her take the wheel. I felt drained from being in the sun all day. "What do you say to picking up Chinese or barbecue, so you won't have to cook? I'm beat and I bet you are, too."

"Barbecue sounds good. I can always cook for you at the beach house."

We stopped at a local hot spot on the way into Panacea and decided to eat there when we realized that most of the patrons were dressed like us. A rack of ribs with all the trimmings shared between us had us stuffed to the point of misery.

"I can tell that dating you is going to force me to start working out much harder," Jade said. "I've eaten more in the past couple of weeks than I have in a month."

I dabbed at the corner of her mouth with my napkin. "You needn't worry. You'll get your exercise with me." I meant from all the beach combing we were going to do, but when I saw the sparkle in her eyes, I didn't correct myself.

"Do you…would you consider dating anyone else besides me?"

"Jade, I'm so enamored with you, I can't look at anyone else. I think what's happening between us is pretty special, don't you?"

"Yes, I do. So it's fair to say we're exclusive?"

I nodded and smiled. "Going steady or whatever you want to call it."

She touched my hand, and I felt utter bliss.

Chapter 19

"You're not serious." Miranda looked between me and Marty. I thought she was going to cry.

Marty reached over and took her hand. "This is Angel's call, baby."

"I've been in Deb's life a lot longer than Angel." Miranda's face flushed red as she looked angrily at us.

I felt terrible for her. Marty had spoken with Angel and given her the name of the nutritionist Miranda was referred to by one of her emergency physician friends. Angel had taken it from there and did the consult alone. She'd already tried to reach Deb, and when that failed, she asked for reinforcements—Marty and me. In Angel's words, "Miranda was too confrontational and too much like Deb."

"I say this with all the love in my heart," Marty began, "but you're like a bulldozer sometimes. A lovable bulldozer."

"So you're saying I'm pushy." Miranda folded her arms.

"You've been great for me, just the friend I needed," I said. "But let's be honest, you and Deb have always argued and competed. She'll say something to spark your ire, and the fight will be on."

Miranda reluctantly agreed. "What time will she be here?" she asked with resignation.

Marty looked at her watch. "In about thirty minutes, then we'll go see Deb."

My stomach turned at the thought. I wished it had been me who pissed Deb off, so I could be excused from the meeting.

Miranda nodded and stood. "I'm going to the gym, but I want to see both of you when you get back."

Angel looked haggard when she arrived. She promptly dissolved into tears when Marty hugged her. "My stomach has been upset all day." She looked at me and Marty. "I may have to stay with one of y'all after the evening is over."

"Let's not go into this expecting the negative," Marty said as she sat next to her.

"What advice has the therapist given?" I asked too nervous to sit with them.

"Not to go on the offensive." Angel ran a shaking hand through her hair. "That's why I thought it wouldn't be a good idea for Miranda to be in on this. I hope I didn't offend her." She looked at Marty, who simply smiled. "She also said not to do it in a public place in respect to Deb's privacy. We should be positive and compassionate and encourage her to seek help. It will only work if it's her idea."

"And if none of this helps?" I asked.

I watched as a tear streaked Angel's face. "The doctor spent a long time preparing me for that. Ultimately, it will be Deb's choice, and there may come a time when I have to step out of the way, all of us, actually." Angel sniffed as she accepted a tissue from Marty. "Enabling takes many forms. I didn't realize I'd been doing that. Turning a blind eye to things and accepting excuses are the most obvious." She wiped her eyes and looked pitiful. "Another more aggressive intervention may have to be done if we can't get her to consider treatment. But I can't even begin to consider that right now."

"What've you already told her?" Marty asked.

"That she's dangerously thin, and I think she's taking the diet to a dangerous level. We had a terrible fight after I found all the laxatives she'd been stockpiling, so I've been hesitant to confront…that particular issue."

Marty looked at me. "So we'll be gentle, but persuasive. No confrontations, no judgmental attitudes."

I nodded, and we embarked on our grim task.

Deb seemed surprised to see us when we walked in behind Angel, but that look of surprise quickly changed to disgust, and I knew we were in for a wild ride. I missed Miranda then. Angel went straight to Deb and threw her arms around her neck, but Deb's gaze met mine, and I felt my insides turn to jelly.

Angel took her by the hand. "Marty and Sloan wanted to come by and see how you're doing." Deb allowed Angel to lead her to the den, but she didn't take a seat.

Marty and I exchanged glances as we sat, but neither of us looked relaxed. "You feel like we're ganging up on you," Marty said gently.

Deb leveled her gaze on Angel. "Wouldn't you?"

"Deb, you're beautiful. We've always loved you, and we always will. And as people who love you, we're concerned about what's happening to you physically." Marty folded her hands and laid them in her lap. "You've lost an awful lot of weight in a short time."

"So?" Deb moved behind a chair. "I'll gain some back."

"I understand about wanting to lose weight," I said. "We just..." This seemed so stupid to me all of the sudden. We'd been friends for years, and we were all trying to approach this clinically. "This is such bullshit, isn't it?" I couldn't help but smile. Marty and Angel stared at me with raised brows. "We've always been friends. Let's just cut the shit and be honest. I'm worried that you've gone past the point of being able to control this. So, Deb, does this have you by the tail or not?" I asked gently.

I stared into her eyes and waited. She smiled and shook her head. "This is my thing, Sloan. Let me cope with it in my own way."

"But can you without help?"

"I don't need any help, I can handle this myself. I'm not going to some clinic or to see a shrink. I'm not sick if that's what you're all thinking." Deb moved around the chair, her shoulders were up. I gripped the armrest and awaited the impending explosion. She leaned down until we were face to face. "Look me in the eye when I say that I'm not bulimic or anorexic."

My hands moved of their own volition, and I laid them on her arms, my mind locked with hers. Through Deb's eyes, I saw the children circling her taunting and laughing. "Debby dump truck, Debby dump truck. Look out, the wide load is coming." I felt her shame, embarrassment, and pain. Then the vision switched, and I recognized the man she used to work with. "If you'd get off your fat ass for a change and do something with yourself, you'd only be half the pathetic creature you are. Really, how does someone let themselves become such a slob?"

The next vision unfolded. I was in a clothing store looking at all the things she could wear if she were a twelve or even a fourteen. I heard her wonder how she had ever gotten so big. How would she ever lose it all and become human again. And then we were in the bathroom of her home, and I felt her fingers sliding into her throat.

"Are you going to puke?" Deb asked, pulling away.

I clutched my stomach and coughed, tasting bile in the back of my throat. I looked up at Deb. "I understand. I know you felt this was the only way." Deb looked at Marty and Angel. Marty's eyes were wide. I directed my comment to Marty. "I need to be honest with her." She looked frightened and shook her head almost imperceptibly, but I forged ahead, certain that I was making the right decision.

I had another coughing and gagging fit as the memory slowly faded from sight. Angel appeared next to me with a glass of water, and I drank greedily until I felt calm again. When I looked at Deb, she had finally sat on the edge of a chair and was watching me intently. "I know you've been ridiculed all your life. Kids called you Debby dump truck. The man you worked with called you—"

"What did you just say?" Deb asked wide-eyed.

"I was there. I saw the kids picking on you."

"I grew up in Montana. There's no way you were there, Sloan. Have you been digging into my life? Talking to my family?" Her face flushed red.

"No. I...saw it in your mind."

"You saw it in my mind?" Deb's voice rose with each word. She shook her head. "I'm not the one with a problem here. You're fucking nuts." She looked at Marty. "Did you hear what she just said?"

Marty nodded. "It's true. Something happened to her in West Virginia. I would've never believed it if she hadn't have told me a secret that only my mother and I knew."

Deb stared at her for a moment. When she spoke, she was calm, but her voice was cold. "So you're all in on this."

"It's not a joke. I wouldn't screw with you like that, Deb."

"Then take my hand." She stood and thrust it at me. "Take my hand and tell me what I'm thinking." Her face twisted into a sneer.

I sighed long and loud. I was getting used to the unbelieving look of challenge in the eyes of those I revealed my secret to. I couldn't help but be a little hurt that my friends who knew me best had to test me. "All right." I moved to the edge of my chair and looked Deb in the eye, then I took her hand.

My hair felt wet against my neck. My chubby little hands held a stuffed cat by the neck as I watched Deb's sister getting ready for the prom. Her mother was taking rollers out of her long glossy blond hair. "You're so beautiful, Tanya," she was saying. Deb caught her own reflection in the mirror behind her slim sister. Her face was round and full of freckles, the total opposite of her flawless elder sibling. I could hear her thoughts, *I'll never be pretty like her.*

Her mother turned and looked at me. "Fetch the hair spray from the bathroom for me, will you, baby?"

"Shake a chunky leg, Deborah. I'm late enough already," her sister called after her.

Through Deb's eyes, I saw the glass of red Kool-Aid she'd left on the counter earlier. I felt the cool of the glass in my hand, felt the hair spray in the other. I knew what was going to happen before it did because the idea was running wildly through Deb's mind. She pretended to trip just as her mother reached for the spray, and I watched as the red liquid coated the bottom of the dress. Tanya's scream echoed in my mind as I released Deb's hand.

I looked at her and said, "Tanya was getting ready for the prom, and you thought you'd never be pretty like her. After your sister said something hateful, you pretended to trip and intentionally poured red Kool-Aid on her dress."

Deb's face contorted as she stood. I could see the realization of the truth in her eyes. She backed away slowly, looking at me like I was some sort of monster.

"Now you know the truth about me and I know about you," I said softly. "We're friends, we battle our demons together. I'd tried to cope with this alone, and I had to lean on Miranda. I tried to shut myself away and she wouldn't let me, and I'm thankful for it. One day, I hope you'll look back on what we want to do for you and feel the same way."

Deb folded her arms and shook her head. "You're a liar." She turned and shook a finger at Angel and spat out, "You've gone to my mother? I'll never forgive you for this." And then she stormed out of the room, leaving the three of us to stare after her.

"What have you done?" Angel asked miserably. "How could you contact her family behind my back?"

"I swear we didn't." I looked at Marty, who sat stunned, for help.

"We truly didn't." Marty reached for Angel, who moved away from her touch.

She stood and put a trembling hand to her lips. "You might've lost a friend in all of this, but I've built a life with Deb. Don't you realize what you've done to me—to us?"

"Angel, please—"

"No," she said, shaking her head. "Just go. I'll handle this myself." She turned and walked into the guest room. I watched helplessly as she closed the door behind her.

"Let's go." Marty stood and ran a hand through her hair. "Come on, Sloan."

I stood slowly and followed her out the door.

"I'm so sorry." I said after we were on the road. I glanced over at Marty. She was wiping a tear with the back of her hand. I'd taken the wrong step and made a bad situation worse.

"What were you thinking?"

"Easy, Miranda." Marty put a hand to her arm and looked at

me. Her expression was a mix of compassion and aggravation. I slid lower in my chair.

"I should've ignored Angel and gone with y'all." She pointed to me and looked at Marty. "She's like a loaded weapon. Someone has to keep a handle on her."

"Thanks a lot," I said as anger surged through me. "I have my own mind. I'm not some sort of freaky tool you can use whenever you want!"

"That's not what I meant." Miranda softened her tone. "I just know what you're thinking, and before you got yourself into trouble, I could've—"

"That's exactly what you meant. You're affirming it with every word you say, so shut up."

"All right." Marty put her hands up to silence us both. "We can't turn on each other, too." She took Miranda by the hand. "Sloan did what she thought was best in the moment. We weren't getting anywhere with Deb. She took a shot, and unfortunately, missed."

Miranda looked at me. "I'm sorry," she said as she reached for my hand.

I pulled away, unwilling to expose myself to her emotions. "I can't take anymore of anyone's feelings. I have enough of my own to deal with." I got up and grabbed my keys. "I just need some time." Marty called after me, but I kept going. Once I was in the safety of my own car and on the road where no one could see or hear me, I let out a yell of anger and frustration, but tears wouldn't come.

I shook my head at the irony of it all. Of everyone I associated with, I was the one who did not deal well with emotion. Even Deb could be a compassionate listener when one of the group was grappling with something. I'd always shied away, feeling I had nothing to offer because up until recently, I couldn't allow myself to feel anything.

But with this new...thing, the floodgates were open and all the feelings I kept neatly organized were free flowing, and all were vying for my attention. Add to that the feelings of everyone around me, and I was lost in a world of overwhelming...shit.

Chapter 20

Miranda walked into my store the next morning looking contrite. "You didn't deserve what you got from me last night," she said as she leaned on my counter. "I'm sorry."

"Not half as sorry as I am for messing everything up with Deb." I looked down at the necklace I was trying to braid for Jade and realized it looked like a conglomeration of knots. I tossed it aside and folded my arms. "I thought it was the only way to get through to her."

"If I had been in your shoes, I would've done the same thing." Miranda picked up Jade's necklace and started undoing the mess I'd made of it. "I was pissed last night at being cut out of the loop, and I took it out on you. Sloan, you didn't mess up anything. It's a screwed-up situation to begin with."

"And I made it worse." I held up a hand when Miranda tried to interject. "Now Angel is mad at me—at us—because she thinks we went behind *her* back and talked to Deb's family. You'd think the truth would make everything clear, but it doesn't when we all have something to hide. You know what the worst part of it is?" Miranda looked up at me. "I understood what Deb was going through. She's been overweight all her life, and nothing has worked for her but this. She feels normal for the first time, and she's killing herself. Jade has the perfect body, and though it keeps her employed, it works against her. We go to the gym and torture ourselves to look and feel better. But not one of us is truly happy with what's on the outside because we do it for everyone else."

"Plastic surgery is booming," Miranda said with a shrug.

"The bad thing is, I can empathize with Deb now. She just

wants to be what she considers normal, and I understand that. I can hide what I do, but she can't hide her weight." I shook my head. "Isn't it ironic, she wants to be my size, and I want to have a relationship like the one she has with Angel?"

"You're on your way, though." Miranda laid the once-mangled mess of Jade's necklace on the counter. "When Jade looks at you, there are stars in her eyes, and you look exactly the same."

I smiled for the first time that morning as I thought of Jade and how lucky I was. "It's funny when I look at her, I don't see that finely tuned body or that beautiful face anymore. I see the woman she is inside, and it turns me inside out." My smile faded. "I wouldn't have given her half a chance if she didn't look like she did. I would've never known the woman she truly is. What does that say about me?"

"I'd say you're learning not to judge on looks alone, and it took you going half to death to evolve."

"What did you ever see in me? I was so shallow. How could you tolerate me?"

Miranda smiled ruefully. "That's a stupid question. We grew up together, and I've always known the person you're only coming to know now. You never gave yourself a chance. Underneath all that self-protectiveness is the woman you really are, and you're finally letting her out."

"Yeah, well, she's killing me with her feelings. Sometimes, she's a real pain in the ass."

Miranda chuckled. "Good."

Chapter 21

Between Deb's intervention and Jade's work schedule, we didn't see each other much during the week. So when Jade's old truck pulled beneath the pilings of the beach house, it was a sweet reunion. I expected a quick kiss, then she'd sprint up the stairs to see our new digs for the week, but she surprised me when she pulled me into her arms and kissed me until I was breathless. "I've missed you." She tried to stroke the hair out of my eyes as it was perpetually buffeted by the wind coming off the water. "I've looked forward to this time with you more than anything I can remember."

"Me too." I held the key up. "Just me, you, and the beach."

Jade grinned and swiped it from my hand. She was up the stairs in a shot, leaving me laughing in her wake. I climbed up slowly as her feelings swirled within me—affection, arousal, bliss.

As I walked in, she looked over her shoulder while she stood in front of the sliding glass doors in the back of the house. I could see past her to the water. My mind made a mental snapshot. If someone else were to be able to see into my mind, they'd see this first and feel the warmth that passed through me head to toe.

"Have you peeked into the bedrooms yet?" I asked as I wrapped my arms around her waist.

"No, I was waiting on you for that." I felt her curiosity, nervousness, her fear of pushing too far too soon.

I kissed her shoulder and squeezed her tighter. "I'd like to sleep in the same bed with you." I felt her relax. "Whatever happens will happen when we both want it to. I want you to know I didn't bring you here in hopes of having sex. I just want all the time I can get with you."

"Me too." I felt the truth of her words pass through me.

"Let's unpack and start enjoying this place." I gave her a squeeze and let her go. We were in a race down the stairs, and she beat me by a mile. I watched the muscles of her bare arms flex as I hooked bag after bag on her hands. "That's too much to carry up the stairs."

"Give me two more and I'll go." I dug out the lightest ones I could find and put them on her hands. She rolled her eyes and headed back up the stairs without effort.

It seemed like it took us forty trips to unload the groceries and our personal items. I felt like I'd run a marathon as I put away the food in the pantry and Jade loaded the fridge with the perishables. She began opening the drawers and cabinets.

"This place has all the comforts of home." She moved past the bar that divided the kitchen from the living room. "Satellite TV, VCR, DVD player, and a shitload of lesbian movies and books."

"Lesbian owned and operated," I said as I came out of the pantry. "From what Miranda says, they rent predominantly to our kind."

Jade ran her fingers over a statue of a mermaid sitting on the bookshelf. "I really like this."

I made a mental note to get one the next time I placed my order for supplies. It would be a great gift to remind her of the week we were going to share. "Let's pick a room." Jade followed behind me as I opened the door closest to the kitchen. The stark white bedspread matched the walls, making the colorful mermaid that hung on the wall over the bed stand out. The rich wood of the bedside tables matched that of the dresser, contrasting with the brightness of the room. Jade walked over the colorful rug at the foot of the bed and opened the shutters.

"This is a sliding glass door. We can sleep with it open and listen to the waves," she said excitedly.

The notion hit us at the same time, and we raced to the other side of the house to look at the other bedroom. It was decorated much the same and had sliding glass doors that opened onto the deck. "Oh, decisions," I said dramatically.

Jade opened the door and let the ocean breeze fill the room.

"Let's use both. We'll start off in the other one, then sleep in this one tomorrow night. Whichever has the most comfortable bed wins."

"I love your logic. Now let's explore the beach."

We both let out a squeal of excitement as we went onto the screened porch, then onto the deck. I followed Jade down two flights of stairs to a wooden walkway that led to the sand. She took my hand as we walked to the water's edge and let the waves lap at our feet.

"This is bliss," Jade said with a smile as she looked out over the water, then turned to me. "Thank you so much for making this happen."

"It would be fair to say *we* made this happen."

"We work well together then." Jade looked at me and sighed. "I'm hungry."

"Look," I said seriously. "Since we're on vacation, can't the diet be on vacation, too? I'm not saying have an all-out pig fest, but maybe fudge just a little?"

Jade's brow rose. "Interesting choice of words. Do you have fudge hidden in the kitchen?"

"Only if you count the stripe in the ice cream."

"You bought ice cream?"

I shrugged. "And cones."

She planted a hand on her hip and narrowed her eyes. "All things in moderation, but—"

"We could eat it now," I said excitedly. "If we wait until after dinner, it'll be late."

"Interesting logic."

I took off running for the stairs. Jade yelled something, but I didn't hesitate as I took them two at a time. As I started up the second flight, Jade was halfway up the first laughing as she climbed. She'd caught up with me by the time I got to the pantry and ripped the door open. When I came out with the cones, she had her hand on the freezer door. "Nothing fattening for dinner, right?" she said, barely breathing heavy from the mad dash.

"I was thinking Mexican. Guacamole with chips and fajitas."

Jade pressed the heel of her hand to her forehead. "Being around you is one temptation after the other."

I moved around her and found an ice cream scoop in one of the drawers. "We'll run on the beach and work it off."

"I want two scoops," Jade said as she retrieved the ice cream from the freezer.

"That's the spirit."

We took our cones out to the deck and watched long strings of pelicans glide over the water. Every now and then, one of us would point out a crab or a bird on the beach. There were a few people who passed by hunting for shells or just walking. They'd wave and we'd do the same.

"You ever notice that people are friendlier in places like this?" Jade asked. "If we were in town and passed someone in a parking lot or store, we wouldn't say hello."

"I think we realize that we're all enjoying the same thing. Like, 'Hello, I'm in paradise, you found it, too.'"

Jade laughed. "I guess so." She slapped at her arm. "Gnats have found our paradise, too."

"I noticed they were bad when we were on the beach. I think they live in the seaweed washed up on the shore. If I were a gnat, I'd live here, too, and I'd definitely bite you, or maybe just ride around on your shoulder."

"Wow, your romantic side is really coming out." Jade put a hand to her cheek. "I may swoon."

I chuckled. "When we first met, I thought you had no sense of humor at all."

"I had my gym face on," Jade said. "All business, baby. Speaking of business, when do we start cooking?"

I took the last bite of my cone and chewed slowly, savoring the sweetness. "I guess this doesn't qualify as food to you?"

"This?" She held up the tiny bottom of her cone and popped it in her mouth. "Not even an appetizer."

"I guess we better start dinner and feed the savage beastie before she goes wild and tears up the place."

We munched on fresh guacamole while Jade cut up the bell

pepper and onions, and I prepared the meat for the grill. I'd pre-sliced and put it into the marinade that morning before I packed. The steak was sure to be good and tender. "How about I open a bottle of wine? That's healthy, right?"

"Already did when you went down to light the grill." She pointed to the kitchen table where the bottle and two glasses sat waiting.

"Corrine Verner, I do believe you're a keeper."

She looked surprised by the comment and smiled. "I hope so."

I stole a quick kiss, then went down to the grill and put the meat on to cook. A cool breeze blew in off the water, and the spices from the meat filled my senses. "How lucky am I?" I said aloud. Less than a month before, I felt like my life was over, and in a way, it was. My emptiness had been replaced with the sweetness of hope and joy. I refused to search out the negatives, the what-ifs, even though a tiny voice deep in my subconscious reminded me that happy times were short-lived.

A pair of long beautiful legs caught my eye as Jade made her way down the stairs slowly. In one hand, she carried something rolled in foil, in the other, a glass of wine. The wind lifted her hair and blew it all around her face. She was absolutely lovely, but it was the way she looked at me that made my knees weak. I was her sole focus. I wanted to touch her then and confirm what I suspected, hoped. I wondered if she saw the same in my eyes—happiness, trust, desire, and the stirring of love.

She laid the foil on the grill. "I thought the onions and peppers would taste better if they cooked with the meat. "And I thought we could share this." She held the glass to my lips, and I took a sip of the wine. I leaned in with it still on my lips and kissed her. If I had to relive one moment in my life for eternity, I was fairly certain that was it because I'd never been happier.

"Can I tell you something?" Jade said later as we finished dinner on the porch.

I looked at her expectantly.

"I'm a little drunk."

I blinked as it settled in. I had no idea what she was going to say, but that certainly wasn't it. I suppose it was the backdrop that led me to believe it was going to be something profound and romantic. The sun was setting, and the sky was streaked with purple and orange. The candlelight in the middle of the table danced in the reflection of our glasses. Gulls sang somewhere off in the distance. "Hey, I'm toasted" didn't seem to fit.

"Are you really?" I looked at her glass and tried to remember how many she'd had.

She nodded. "The glass I had at your house was the first in probably five or six years."

Her somber expression gave me pause. Perhaps she'd had a problem with alcohol and my penchant for temptation led her to fall off the wagon. "Is there a reason you're not supposed to drink?"

She looked at me with her brow furrowed for second, then her eyes opened wide. "Oh, no. I just don't drink." She shrugged. "I don't have much of a tolerance for it, which should be fairly obvious."

"Then that's okay," I said with relief. "There's nothing wrong with getting a little…buzzed."

She averted her gaze and looked out at the water. "I don't want to be…buzzed the first time we're together. If that's what you had planned…I mean I didn't want you to think I was rejecting you if…" She tossed her napkin on the table. "I'm sorry. I knew I should've paid more attention."

"You've picked up my habit of babbling when you're nervous." I reached over and ran a fingertip down the side of her jaw. "Don't apologize. I could never be mad at you for something like that. If anything, I think it's really sweet that you don't want to be drunk. I've dated quite a few women that wanted to be shit-faced before they got into bed with me."

She took my hand and kissed the back of it. "Thank you."

"I'm gonna clear the table. Why don't you make yourself comfy on the couch and we'll watch a movie?"

"Nope, I'm gonna help." Jade stood suddenly and picked up her plate. I followed behind her and chuckled softly at the zigzag she cut across the room.

"Oh, I wish your clients could see you now."

She looked over her shoulder as she put her plate in the sink. "If you take out your phone to record any of this, I'll..." She bit her lip. "I have...no idea. I'm a little slow on the uptake right now." She wiped at her face and broke into a fit of giggles. "I've never been drunk before."

"Never? You're telling me you've never been smashed at least once?" I moved beside her and rinsed my plate. "Methinks you lie."

"Me...I think...no, I've never been." She wagged a finger at me. "See, you're all sorts of temptations."

"Well, I think you should have some more wine then. I'd like to see your first full-on drunk."

Her expression turned serious. "My dad was a drinker. That's what turned me off of it." Jade shook her head like she was trying to shake off the thought. "What movie are we seeing?"

I stuffed the cork into the wine bottle and set it off to the side. "You pick." I watched her move unsteadily into the living room and look at the selection as I wiped down the counters.

"This!" She held up a box.

I hoped it wasn't something with a lot of steamy sex in it. The wine had dulled my inhibitions, and I was not in the mood for a cold shower. I walked over and took the box from her hand. "*Rocky and Bullwinkle*? Absolutely."

We lay on each end of the L-shaped couch with our heads on pillows in the middle. Jade reached out and took my hand. She was asleep before Boris Badenov came up with his first diabolical plan for the moose and squirrel.

Chapter 22

I awoke with a start. Alone on the couch, I sat up and listened for Jade, wondering if she'd gotten up during the night and went to one of the beds. Quietly, I stretched and yawned, then tiptoed through the house. Jade wasn't there. After a trip to the bathroom, I walked out onto the porch. Dark clouds loomed on the horizon. I hoped that I was looking at the tail end of a storm system that was moving away.

"Good morning."

I looked down and saw Jade standing on the beach, waving up at me. When I walked onto the deck, I noticed that she was dripping wet. "Did you swim or is that sweat?"

She looked pleased with herself. "I ran all the way down to the state park and back. I'll go again if you want to join me."

"Oh, no," I said with a laugh. "Workouts are for the afternoon. Right now, it's coffee time."

"Better drink it fast if you want some time in the sun." Jade sprinted up the stairs. "According to the report I saw on TV, it's supposed to rain."

"You've already run and watched TV this morning? What time is it?"

She looked down at her watch. "It's nine, and you sleep like the dead."

I rubbed at the kink in my neck. "You're not hungover?"

"I had a tiny headache this morning, but after a couple of Tylenol and two bottles of water, I felt okay." She smiled. "The run did me good."

"You're insane." I turned and went back into the house with

Jade on my heels. "Beautiful, but totally insane. I'm gonna put on some coffee and change into my swimsuit."

"I should shower first." Jade tugged at her wet tank top.

"Why? You're just gonna slather yourself with sunscreen and bug repellent." I nearly spilled the coffee grounds I was measuring as she pulled off her shirt. I'd seen her in a pair of shorts and sports bra more times than I could count, but the sight still took my breath away.

"You have a good point. I'll just go rinse off for now."

I watched her walk away, wishing I'd bought the kind of sunscreen that you had to rub on instead of spray.

"Now this is the life." Jade stretched out on her lounge chair. Her skin glistened in the sun as she reached down and pulled a bottle of water out of a metal pail that we'd filled with ice. Her chair was close to mine so we could share my iPod. She had one ear bud and I had the other. "I like this woman's voice. Who are we listening to?"

"Brandi Carlile. She's one of my favorites."

"She's raspy and emotional," Jade said. "You can tell she feels what she's singing."

My eyes were closed, Brandi was singing in my ear, the sun was warm on my skin, and something hit my stomach that was so shocking I nearly wet myself. I bolted upright as a chunk of ice landed on my chair. I looked back at Jade, who was looking as innocent as she could manage behind her dark glasses. "So that's how it's gonna be."

"Huh?" Jade pulled the bud from her ear. "Sorry, I didn't hear you."

"I said, it's time for lunch. We're having seaweed sandwiches. Ever have one?" I reached down and grabbed a glob of the stuff. The gnats swarmed and nearly chewed my arm off.

"Sloan, if you put that on me, I'll totally freak out." Jade scrambled to get out of her chair. "You have no idea what's living in there."

"Maybe a crab, maybe the Loch Ness Monster's baby, but they'll all be happy living in your shorts." I sprinted after her as she ran screaming like a sissy girl down the beach. I was laughing so hard, I could barely keep up. Her tough-girl persona was totally shattered. "Come back here and take it like a woman."

Jade cut close to the water and let me gain on her. I really had no intention of touching her with the seaweed, but when she tripped and went down, the weed and I joined her. The clump of decaying mush landed on her upper arm, and she did freak, arms and legs flailing wildly. My apology sounded insincere coming out between fits of uncontrollable laughter. The battle was on.

Jade grabbed me by the ankle and started dragging me toward the water. "Don't you...Jade, I don't go into anything I can't see the bottom of." I twisted and turned, trying to break her grasp. When the water met my butt, it felt like ice. I grabbed Jade around the leg and tried to pull her down before she could get me any deeper. When that didn't work, I grabbed a handful of wet sand and tried to stuff it in her shorts. She lost her footing and went down on her knees. We were both laughing hysterically as we tried to put sand in each other's shorts and bras.

Jade fell silent and looked past my shoulder. Still laughing, I followed her gaze and turned to see Jacquelyn standing on the beach with her arms folded. Her displeasure was obvious. "I distinctly remember you saying you did not date your clients."

I looked back at Jade, unsure of whether I should point out that I wasn't a client, but what I really wanted to do was tell Jacquelyn it wasn't really any of her business. Jade's stunned expression slowly changed into one of indifference. "As a rule, I don't. If I had been honest and told you that I was involved with someone, would it have made a difference?"

Jacquelyn looked at me pointedly. "No, it wouldn't have."

"What're you doing here?" I asked as anger surged through me.

"I live here." Jacquelyn looked back at Jade. "I'll see you Monday."

"Actually, you'll be seeing Jim. I'm off Monday," Jade said. "You'll like him. He's single and dates quite a few clients."

Jacquelyn shot me a smile, then looked back at Jade. "I'll see you Tuesday then."

I didn't wait for Jacquelyn to get out of earshot before saying, "pretentious bitch."

Jade grinned as she pulled a piece of seaweed from my chest. "She's just jealous. Not everyone finds a pearl on the beach."

"Oh, that was really sweet, but I think you're just saying that to avoid having a handful of sand shoved down your butt crack."

Jade opened her mouth to retort when the first raindrop hit her squarely in the forehead. We both jumped up and ran to the chairs. The rain started to pound as I grabbed my iPod and she grabbed the towels. We used the water hose to rinse off the sand, and between the wind and rain, we were freezing.

"You shower first," Jade said between chattering teeth when we walked onto the porch.

"There are two bathrooms. If we're quick, we'll both have hot water." We went our separate ways into the bathrooms. After I'd bathed, I wanted to stand under the hot spray until it ran cold but got out quickly, afraid that I'd take the hot water from Jade.

As I combed the tangles from my hair, thunder rocked the small house. It seemed to vibrate with every crash. I looked up at the light and wondered how long the power would stay on. My answer came a heartbeat later. I wrapped a towel around myself, cursing the fact that I'd picked the bathroom that didn't adjoin the room with our clothes.

The door to the bathroom that Jade had chosen was closed, so I felt safe creeping into the room with half of my rear end hanging out from beneath the towel. Jade lay in the bed on her stomach, the sheet at her waist revealing her bare back. She was staring out at the storm as it pounded the house. "I was hoping you would come to me," she said, her voice barely audible over the storm.

Heat rushed over me like the lightning flashing outside, burning and calling every nerve ending to life. I swallowed hard as I walked slowly to the bed. She didn't move as I dropped the towel and crawled in beside her. I lay on my side and reached out to touch her skin. My hand hovered as I mentally prepared myself.

This wasn't going to be like all the other times when the other person's feelings meant nothing to me. My goal had been to please and be pleased, but my heart was never engaged. It felt like such a monumental step for me. This moment, this act was going to change everything. I exhaled softly and let my fingers drift over skin smooth as silk.

I'd hoped to lose myself in the place where my mind and body were centered on sensation, but that was not the case. My body was responding to the delight beneath my fingers, but my brain was pushing for its own connection. I blinked rapidly as images formed in the peripheral. My want for her confused and frustrated me. Mind, body, and soul clamored for its own connection, each refusing to be deprived. A soft groan crossed my lips as it occurred to me that I might not be strong enough to close the door between my mind and Jade's private thoughts.

As I began to withdraw, Jade's emotions pushed through—fear and desire, need and insecurity. But above all those feelings, there was affection so strong and sweet. I could feel her hesitancy to put a name to it just as I had. I absorbed her feelings and let them intertwine with mine. The images in the corner of my mind's eye darkened and receded as I caressed her back. Muscles moved beneath warm velvety skin.

Jade rolled beneath my hand onto her back. She draped an arm over her head and looked deep into my eyes, searching for what I gleaned in a touch.

"This is just the beginning of something I know in my heart has no end," I said softly. I took her hand and pressed it against my chest. "You can't feel what I'm feeling, so I have to tell you, show you, and I've never been good at that. If you'll trust me, I will never let you down, never let you go. Don't move," I said when her hand moved and gripped the back of my neck. I ran my hand down her chest between her breasts and across her stomach. "I just want to touch you for a minute."

She relaxed, but the muscles in her stomach quivered as my fingers drifted over them. I pressed my palm over her hip bone, then slid it down a silky thigh. My feelings came to the forefront then—arousal and longing.

Jade's gaze stayed locked with mine as I moved my hand slowly up the inside of her thigh. The higher I went, the hotter her skin became. She grasped my hand when it reached the bend of her leg. A small smile creased her lips as she rolled over, pinning me to the bed.

"What do you feel when you touch me?" She looked into my eyes.

"Smooth skin, taut muscle," I said with a grin of my own, then said seriously, "adored."

"You are," she said before kissing me.

So many sensations hit me at once, the softness of her mouth, her tongue moving against mine, the heat of her skin, the slow grind of her hips, and passion that mingled with mine and made my head swim. Breathless, I broke the kiss and moved to her neck where I nibbled and kissed the sweet-smelling skin. The movement of her hips became more insistent before she devoured my mouth again.

Jade was moving into that place where thought ceases and the mind is only aware of sensation. Her fear slipped away, and the craving for a connection that transcended sex flowed through her. I had thought making love would be difficult with my ability, but it made it so much more intense. I was experiencing all of Jade, mind and body.

I felt the muscles in her stomach tense against mine. She tried to pull away, but I wrapped my legs tighter around her and whispered in her ear, "Don't stop." She groaned and buried her face in my neck. The muscles in her back felt like iron under my touch. My entire body quivered with excitement as her orgasm grew nearer. She stopped moving, and I felt the breath go out of her in a shudder. Her mind engaged with her body again, and I felt her affection for me so strong it made me weak.

My body responded to her kisses and strokes of its own volition, but my mind fought for dominance, once again trying to process each emotion and sensation. Jade's tongue and teeth on my nipple made me gasp, and for a second, I told my brain to shut the hell up, but as she began her descent, I wove my hands in her hair.

"What's wrong?" Jade's eyes reflected fear and disappointment as I felt it flow through her touch.

"I need..." I let out a long sigh and rolled her over onto her back. "I need to touch you for a little longer."

"We don't have to do this if you're not ready." Jade looked into my eyes. "I mean it."

I ran my tongue up the center of her chest and listened with great pleasure to her sharp intake of breath. "I'm ready," I said before I grazed my teeth across her nipple. "My mind just won't shut off long enough for me to relax and enjoy. Distract me, talk to me."

"How about music? I've never been good at talking dirty I—Oh." Jade's eyes flew open wide when I put my leg between hers and thrust against her.

I couldn't help but grin. "You were saying?"

"I gi...I giggle when I try to be dirty."

I moved both legs between hers and watched as her eyes closed. "I guess phone sex is out of the question." A slight smile spread across her lips, then disappeared when I began a slow grind. "So tell me what you want to do tomorrow."

"This."

"Elaborate." I made a string of kisses and soft bites down her chest to her stomach.

"Well," she began breathlessly. "I would like to go shelling and—oh, fuck." Jade's body cleared the bed when I ran my tongue over the bend of her leg where it joined her hip.

"I thought you couldn't talk dirty." She didn't respond as I nibbled my way down one thigh to her knee. Her arousal was so intense, it matched mine, and the mingling of both in my mind made my heart pound. I watched the rapid rise and fall of her chest as I kissed my way up her other thigh.

"Don't tease me," she rasped and grabbed my hair. I heard her whisper my name in the distance as I slid my tongue inside her. The taste and the feel pushed all conscious thought from my mind. For the first time since I'd awoken in the hospital, my mind was blank and my body took over. I couldn't get enough. I devoured her until she screamed out my name throatily and pushed me away.

I didn't know what was happening to me until I felt my back

hit the bed. Jade was above me, then I felt her fingers sliding into me and her other hand gripping mine above my head. "Fuck me, Jade, make me feel it." I wasn't thinking, only feeling her move inside of me. My whole body was awash in sensation. She had me saying things I didn't even understand. I felt her shift and put more of her weight on me when she withdrew her fingers and lightly grazed my clit. I could only gasp her name, but she knew what I wanted and what I needed, and she gave it.

My back would've arched off the bed, but Jade had me pinned in the position she wanted. No sooner than the mind-shattering orgasm subsided, she started working me again. "I can't take it."

"Yes, you can. I'll go slow."

I didn't want to go slow, but I couldn't stand the intensity, either. I couldn't move or squirm out of her grasp. For a split second, the helplessness scared me, but fear turned into something else when I realized she wouldn't hurt me and would let me free if I asked…and I wasn't going to. With each slow stroke, I felt it building. "Trust me," she whispered and centered her weight on my chest until I could hardly breathe. When I came, it was blinding.

"Are you back on earth?" Jade was propped up on one elbow, sporting a satisfied grin.

"Not sure…parts of me are…I think."

"We need water," she said as she climbed from the bed. "Can't have you dehydrated before we really begin."

I watched her go thinking I was way out of my league.

Chapter 23

I awoke in an empty bed. The smell of coffee filled my senses, and I stretched out the kinks. I had always prided myself as an energetic lover, but Jade had me beat by miles. I was fairly certain that I'd gotten more of a workout the previous evening than anytime at the gym, though far more pleasurable. I got up and pulled on a pair of shorts and a T-shirt. Jade was on the porch with a book, so I brushed my teeth, filled my cup with coffee, and joined her.

"Good morning," she said as I leaned down to kiss her. I hesitated when she picked up her cup and drank from it instead. I took a seat thinking that maybe she hadn't had a chance to brush her teeth and didn't want me in her face.

She set the book on the table without marking her place. Her expression was solemn as she stared out at the water. My heart sank. Surely, she couldn't be having regrets. I'd sensed every emotion that passed through her the night before. She was content and happy before we drifted off to sleep. "Is something wrong?"

She didn't look my way. "You promised to always tell the truth, right?"

"Yes."

"You didn't...we were in contact a lot last night." She exhaled loudly and bit her bottom lip. "You didn't go into my mind, did you?"

Stunned by the question, I didn't readily respond, then anger took the place of surprise. "I gave you my word I wouldn't willingly do that."

Jade shook her head. "I'm not saying you would do it

on purpose. What I want to know is if you would tell me if it happened by mistake."

I sank back in my chair. "No, I didn't see anything, and yes, I would tell you if I did. I would pull away from you no matter what we were doing."

Neither of us said anything. Instead, we sat there staring at the Gulf drinking coffee. The previous night had been magical. I never would've imagined that we'd start the day like this. It confused and angered me. "I imagine that being with me is a real challenge to your trust. I'm sure there are memories locked away in the back of my mind that I would be uncomfortable with someone looking in on, so I'm trying to empathize with you. I respect your privacy." I bit my lip and rubbed my brow. The tone of my voice was edged with an anger I couldn't rein in.

"There are a lot of things I want to tell you, but I need to do it on my own time." She looked at me. "I've never killed or harmed anyone, and I've never been arrested, it's nothing along those lines. It's just something personal to me…and I've never told anyone."

My anger began to ebb. I smiled when I thought back to what Miranda asked me the first time I peeked into Jade's mind. She'd be relieved to know that Jade had not committed murder. "I'm content to wait on anything you have to tell me."

"Thanks."

I watched a pair of fins moving through the water every so often. The dolphins would come near enough to the surface for me to see the tops of their heads. Jade was watching them, too, but said nothing. I couldn't make sense of her mood. If anything, I expected making love to draw us closer, not build a wall between us. The urge to be alone came on strong, so I could nurse my damaged feelings.

"You want to go for a run?" Jade asked.

"Uh, no." I mustered up a smile and glanced at her. "It's too early for me, but you go. You wanna borrow my iPod?"

"No, thanks," she said as she stood. "I'll be back soon."

I watched her go, feeling empty. She started in the direction that Jacquelyn went the day before, then turned and ran the other way. I sighed, thinking that was a good sign. I'd promised that I'd never pry into her thoughts, but for the moment, I wished I could see what was causing her odd behavior.

She'd given herself to me willingly and completely the night before, but that morning, she was a stranger. It felt as though she was deliberately trying to sabotage what we'd begun. My feelings were at war with what I thought I knew. She wanted me as much as I wanted her, or at least I'd thought so.

I went inside and sat on the sofa as I replayed our conversation. I figured it made sense for her to be concerned. We'd been in physical contact more in those few hours than we had since we'd met. Then again, she hadn't let me kiss her that morning, so she must be feeling…something she didn't want me to know. I buried my head in my hands and groaned at the irony. This was the very first time I'd ever wanted to wake up with someone, and apparently, she didn't feel the same.

I found my cell phone and gave Miranda a call, but it went to voice mail. She was on shift and probably running a call. "Hey, just checking in. I'll call you later." I flipped it closed and headed for the shower.

An hour later, Jade came walking up the stairs. Her hair was wet, as well as her clothes. "That was one hell of a run," I said.

She put her arms above her head and paced back and forth until her breathing slowed. "I'm really sorry about earlier." She shook her head. "I don't know what got into me. Sometimes, you're almost too good to be true."

I squinted against the sun as I looked up at her. "I think the same about you."

Either Jade was nervous or the adrenaline push was making her hyper. She circled the deck three times. "I'd like to take a shower and start this day over." She wiped the sweat from her face with both hands. "Can we?"

"I'd like that."

She smiled slightly and moved past me to the door. "I'll be right back."

I looked back out over the water, feeling uneasy. Though Jade had apologized, I was still hurting, and the pain was very close to the surface. The notion that we might not be as perfect as I hoped crept around the fringes of my mind, even though I tried to deny it. I tried to rationalize every feeling, then tuck it away in a mental box for safe keeping.

She was afraid of giving her heart away. I could relate. Box one filed away. Not only did she have to trust me with her feelings, she had to trust that I would not invade her innermost thoughts. That made perfect sense. I closed the lid on the second box. I'd moved inside to the sofa and was still wrestling with box number three fifteen minutes later when Jade rejoined me.

She leaned down to kiss me softly, slowly. I felt that same sweet affection but fear that was slowly receding. And the lingering effects of something else that lay beyond my reach.

"Can I ask you a very personal question?" I said when she took a seat beside me. I watched a tiny muscle in her jaw tighten as she nodded. "I've never asked about your past relationships. Have you ever been in love?"

Jade looked down at her hands folded in her lap. "You're not going to believe me when I say I don't know."

"Try me."

She turned to face me, but her gaze remained fixed on something beyond my shoulder. "The trainer I told you about, the one that got me into fitness...I developed a huge crush on her. I'd always been attracted to girls, but that was the first time I felt physical desire." Jade blinked and smiled slightly. "I think she knew it and kept me at arm's length. I was only seventeen, she was twenty-eight. The night before my eighteenth birthday, she took me to dinner, and afterward, she kissed me."

"That was your first kiss then?" I asked when she went silent.

Jade looked at me and nodded. "She said, 'This is all I can ever offer you, just a birthday kiss.' My head was swimming when she hugged me and explained that I was too young for her, and she wouldn't take advantage of my youth." Jade looked back down at her hands. "She avoided me after that. It broke my heart, but in time, I realized that she respected me. She could've easily taken advantage, but she didn't. She'll always hold a special place in my heart because of that."

"You never felt that same respect from any of the other women you were involved with?"

Jade smiled and shrugged. "When you put your body on display, you don't attract the sort that is looking for love and respect. I took advantage of that for a while, losing myself in mindless sex. Somewhere along the line, I decided I wanted more, but I kept drawing in the same type of women, hoping to find something different. I never did, and one day, I gave up." She met my gaze. "And then along came you."

I smiled, but when she looked away, I felt it slip from my face. Had I met her a couple of months earlier, I would've been the same type of woman she'd grown tired of.

"Timing is everything, Sloan." Jade looked back at me. "Don't you think so?"

I nodded.

"Do you sometimes feel that this is all just a wonderful dream and the other shoe will fall, and…I mean, neither of us has good track records…but I think we work."

"So…you're just scared, too?"

She nodded. "I have no control. I tried to go into this using my head, but my heart," she smiled, "just has a mind of its own."

The lid on box three closed and drifted away to the place where I kept everything tucked away. With a smile of my own, I said, "I know exactly what you mean." I stood. "Wait here, I'll be right back." I went into the bedroom and fished around in my suitcase until I found what I was looking for. Of all the necklaces I'd made, this one was my finest work, but even still, I thought Jade deserved so much more. I walked back into the living room with it clutched in my hand and sat down.

"I made this for you, but please don't feel like you have to wear it if you don't like it." Jade's eyes widened as she looked down at my clenched fist. "You could always hang it around your rearview mirror, or—"

Jade put a finger to my lips. "If you took the time to make it for me, then it's very special. Open your hand."

I grinned as I uncurled my fingers to reveal the necklace. I'd chosen a tiny whelk shell less than an inch long that looked like someone had sawed it down the middle revealing the chambers inside. The necklace itself was a flat braid on either side of the shell, which was suspended by a silver clasp. "I found the shell the first time we went to St. George Island. I figured since you loved the beach as much as I did, you'd like to have—"

Jade's lips were on mine, the kiss was sweet and tender conveyed absolute joy.

"You have no idea how much this means to me." Her fingers moved reverently over the shell and braid.

"After that kiss," I said breathlessly, "I'm certain I do."

She turned and lifted her hair. "Put it on me."

I did as she asked and was blessed with a huge smile as she turned to face me.

Jade reached over and ran one finger down my arm, leaving a trail of goose flesh behind it. "Tell me what I'm feeling right now."

I closed my eyes and feigned concentration. I didn't need her touch to know what she was feeling because it clearly showed in her eyes. "Amorous," I said with a smile, "very amorous."

"And what else?" She was close. I could feel her breath against my ear, it made me tremble.

Desire coursed through me stronger than my own. My eyes remained closed. I bit my lip. "Incredibly turned on." Her mouth was on mine then as she pushed me down onto the couch. I felt the warmth and the pressure of her body, the taste of her kiss, and a flood of emotion that brought tears to my eyes. She was truly opening to me, and it surprised her equally as much. I felt her trust and just how safe she felt in my arms.

Through touch, I tried to convey everything she meant to me. I caressed her face and her hair and treated her body as though it was the treasure I truly believed it was. I heard her sigh as I kissed her neck and sensed her joy at truly being cherished, desired, and though I had not said it, loved.

I whispered against her skin, "You make me feel so much. I've never wanted to be a part of someone like this. Does it make sense when I say you might be my other half?"

Half To Death

I felt and heard Jade's soft laugh. "Makes perfect sense." Her expression was one of surprise when she raised up on her elbows and noticed the tears that had pooled in the corners of my eyes. "I can't believe I've finally found you. I feel like I've been looking all my life." She covered my face with soft kisses, and when her lips met mine, I felt loved.

We didn't go down to the beach that day, nor did we bother to get dressed.

Chapter 24

An hour before the alarm was set to go off, I awoke with Jade's head on my shoulder and her arms and legs wrapped around me. I needed to go to the bathroom, but she felt too good and was sleeping so soundly I didn't want to disturb her. I closed my eyes and willed my complaining bladder to go back to sleep. I began to dream in vivid colors…at least I thought it was a dream.

I couldn't breathe, couldn't scream. The hands that held me were strong, they hurt, but the physical pain was nothing to compare with the agony burning in my soul. Betrayal cut me so deep, I didn't want to draw my next breath, but I did. When I exhaled, a ragged scream came with it. The sound of it wrenched me from my haze, but I couldn't stop the screams that tore through me.

"Sloan." Jade reached for me. She looked so much like him that I scrambled to get away, kicking at her until I fell onto the floor. "You had a nightmare." She climbed across the bed and looked at me as I curled myself into a tight ball. "Honey," she said as she reached out for me but hesitated.

I was awake. I felt the sand that we'd tracked into the beach house rub into my skin. I saw my suitcase on the floor. I knew where I was, but even still, I felt like I'd been in a time warp and stepped from one room to another. And I could still smell his sweat on my skin. I had no control of the words that began to spill from somewhere deep within. "Why? What's wrong with me?"

Jade shook her head, her brow furrowed in confusion. "There's nothing wrong with you, Sloan. You had a bad dream." She reached for me again. I got up on my hands and knees and crawled away. She had his eyes.

"Why would he do that to me?" I screamed. "Why wouldn't she believe me?"

"Who?" Jade looked as terrified as I felt.

Fear, betrayal, and confusion washed over me in waves. "Dad." It came out in a whisper.

Jade's face paled and fell slack. Her hand trembled as she put her fingers to her chin. "You saw..." She covered her face with her hands.

It wasn't a nightmare. The revelation hit me as hard as if I'd been hit with a bat. My stomach rebelled. I crawled into the bathroom and heaved into the toilet. I ached physically and emotionally. My mind was being battered with one strong emotion after another—self-loathing, bewilderment, hatred. I couldn't be sure if they were my own or Jade's as they pounded me relentlessly. I hid myself between the tub and toilet, rocking back and forth, counting frantically to escape the never-ending tide of agony.

Something warm enveloped me, hands caressed my ankle, a soft feminine voice called to me. "Sloan, wake up, honey, it's me." I opened my eyes and jerked away from the touch. "It's Miranda, Sloan, wake up." Relief flooded me as I looked up from the bottom of the toilet bowl. Slowly, I raised my head and looked into a familiar face. "You need to get up so we can get you dressed." I wrapped the towel that she had laid over me tighter and took the offered hand.

Miranda led me back to the bedroom and sat me on the bed before she dug through my bag. I looked down at my wrists, expecting to see bruises, and started to cry. Miranda laid my things on the bed and knelt before me. "Did she hurt you?"

I shook my head. "He did." I looked around the room afraid that someone would overhear.

Confusion marred her features. "Who?"

"Jade's father." It came out in a whisper. "I saw...I felt what he did to her." I looked around the room. "Where is she?"

"She's not here," Miranda said soothingly. "Let's get you dressed."

"I...need you to leave the room."

Miranda stood and looked at me oddly. "I've seen you naked a billion times."

"I need you to leave," I said between chattering teeth.

"Okay." She held her hands up and backed away. "I'll be right outside."

I waited for her to close the door and pulled on my clothes quickly, afraid that she would come in and see my nakedness. "I need to go home." Miranda looked at me strangely as I walked shakily into the living room.

"I put some coffee on to brew." She walked over and tried to take my hand, but I pulled away and sank down into a chair at the table. She sat opposite me. "What happened?"

"Where is she?"

Miranda shook her head. "I don't know. She was hysterical when she called and told me to get here as fast as I could. That's about all I could understand." New tears dripped from my eyes and Miranda exhaled shakily. "What happened?"

"I was asleep...I thought I was...maybe just sleeping light, but I saw—felt—what he did to her. I was her." My jaw was trembling so hard, I could barely speak.

Miranda's face flushed. "She was molested."

It nauseated me to hear the word. I nodded as my stomach roiled. "I can't say anymore."

Miranda nodded as she rubbed the bridge of her nose. "You felt her pain, her emotions."

"Yes."

"We need to find her." Miranda banged her hand on the table, making me jump. "I'm sorry," she said and blew out a long breath.

"I can't go with you."

Miranda looked stunned. "Why?"

"I just can't right now." My sobs coalesced into a deep heaving cry. Miranda came around the table and wrapped me in her arms until I calmed. I gripped the lapels on her shirt. "Do this for me. Find her, make sure she's okay. I just need a little time."

"Can I call Marty over to be with you? I don't like the idea of you being alone."

I couldn't stand the idea of seeing anyone. I wanted to shut myself away. "No, I'm going home."

"I'll follow you out, then I'll find Jade, okay?"

My room was dark and familiar. I lay in bed staring up into the darkness, trying to dispel the visions and the accompanying feelings. I was there when she cried herself to sleep, staring at the empty bed across the room. The one her grandmother used to occupy. Jade had felt safe with her there. Her hands were so small as they clutched the covers. I felt her fear, the sting of her mother's denial. As a grown woman, it was almost too much to bear. I had no idea how Jade coped then.

Her parents weren't dead as Jade claimed, although they were dead to her. I remembered looking through her eyes at the house enshrouded in darkness as she crept away in the night never to return. I felt the bitter chill of winter while she camped in a tent hiding and hoping no one would find her. I saw the compassion in a stranger's eyes who offered a young child a job. I felt her stomach tie into knots and heard her ardent prayers as she watched him look over her application where most of the information was falsified.

I was in her body when she ate cold food from a can. When she showered at the gym hoping no one would notice that she did it every morning before opening, then late in the evening. I was there when she scratched up enough money to afford a rat hole of an apartment. I felt the sweat on her palms as she filled out the application to legally change her name from Hutchins to Verner.

I felt her lack of self-worth. I was in her mind when she wondered what she could have done to cause her father to do the things he did. I was there when she pondered what she could've done to stop it. I felt her helplessness when she found the courage to admit what was happening to her mother.

"*You're lying.*" *Her mother's hand shook as she poured herself a drink from the bottle Jade was not to touch.*

"Momma."

"No, Corrine!" Her mother slammed her hand down on the counter. "Stop it now." She pointed angrily at her. "Don't you ever mention this again, not to me, not to anyone. Do you understand?"

I was so angry. I sat up and pounded my pillow with my fists, grinding my teeth until I thought they would break. How could she—they—do this to a child? I was sickened and furious with her father for what he did, but a deep seething hatred for her mother burned in the pit of my stomach. She knew, and she did nothing to stop it.

I'd never contemplated murder, but I wanted to put my hands on these people. I wanted to inflict pain. I wanted to pour into them what I was feeling, what Jade had felt for so many years—but Jade was different. She no longer shared this hostility. She had killed them off in her mind, but I could not. And for that…I resented her.

Chapter 25

"Get up." Miranda opened the blinds and filled the room with light.

I pulled the covers over my head and clamped my eyes shut.

"You're gonna get up, bathe, and eat. You've been locked away in this room for two days." Miranda grabbed the blankets and yanked them from the bed.

"Get out!" I screamed at the top of my lungs. "Get the fuck out and leave me alone."

"Don't you want to know about Jade? Don't you care?" Miranda asked with a tone laced with anger and hurt.

I curled tighter into a ball and clamped my hands over my ears.

She grabbed my feet and yanked my legs. "Get up, Sloan!"

"Motherfucker!" I started kicking and screaming, but Miranda was undaunted. She launched herself onto the bed and covered me with her body until I stilled. Her breath was hot against my ear.

"I won't let you go. I won't let you cave in on yourself." Miranda's tears dripped down on my face. "I know you're in pain, and you want to escape, but you've got to face it for yourself and Jade. I won't let you go. I'll be right here like you've always been for me." We stayed like that until I could no longer bear her weight.

I scrubbed my skin hard in the shower, trying to erase the memory of his touch, his odor. I spent a long time in there, letting the hot water run over my body, hoping it would wash away the powerful anger I felt. In truth, I didn't want it to recede because beneath it lay a pain so sharp I didn't think I could handle it.

"Here." Miranda thrust a towel around the curtain when she heard the water cut off. "I'll turn my back while you dry off and dress, but I'm not leaving."

She'd been a constant shadow since I'd crawled from the bed. She said nothing as I ate a piece of toast and drank a glass of milk. She was waiting. Biding her time until I ate and bathed, then she'd ask all the questions I didn't want to answer.

I brushed past her after I dressed and sank down onto the couch. She followed and sat beside me. "I get it. I understand what you're going through."

"You don't know a fucking thing. You weren't there. In less than an hour, I lived Jade's life. I was…violated right along with her. She's had a lifetime to cope. I've had a couple of days, so give me a fucking break."

"You need help," Miranda said gently. "You need to see someone."

"And tell them what? That I have a *gift* that allows me to live the most painful periods of someone's life? They'll have me committed."

"You could say it was you that was molested," Miranda said calmly. "I imagine the treatment would be—"

"I'm not admitting that! I'm not going to sit in some office and let some stranger pick through my mind. That's pathetic."

I couldn't ignore the pain that filled Miranda's eyes. "I did it, and I am not pathetic." Her eyes narrowed. "You're intentionally caustic because you want to wallow in your pain."

"I am," I said with a nod. "I'm angry and I want to remain so. It's the only thing I can hang on to right now. I don't have to think. I can just be pissed."

Miranda tilted her head to the side, and she regarded me. "Pissed at whom?"

"Isn't the answer obvious?"

"Yeah, it is, but I don't think you realize it." Miranda took a calming breath. "It's Jade you're mad at."

"No." It was a lie, and we both knew it, but to voice it meant I had to own it, and I wasn't ready for that.

Miranda shook her head. "There's so much I don't understand, but you're not being true to me or yourself."

"I can't face her right now. She looks just like her father. It makes it too real."

"She's in a lot of pain. She's kept this secret for years, never telling anyone, and though you didn't do it on purpose, you've forced her to confront old demons. The one person that can truly understand and empathize is you. If you care anything for her, you have to get yourself together and be there for her."

"She admitted it to you?"

Miranda nodded with a grim expression. "What her father did, her mother's denial...I didn't experience it the way you did, but it hurt me, too. Seeing her face, the disconnect as she talked about it has scarred me for life." I looked away, unable to stand the way Miranda looked at me. "You need to talk about it. Release whatever you're holding inside." Miranda cleared her throat. "She said you could talk to me about it. She knows you need to."

"Not right now." I wrapped my arms tight around myself as if to keep it all in. For it all to pass my lips would bring everything into reality. For the moment, I wanted to consider it all a very bad dream.

Miranda stood with a sigh. "I'm going to open up your store. Kaylie's been coming in after school, and I've opened when I could."

"Thank you, I really appreciate it."

"Hey." I turned to look at Miranda as she leaned against the kitchen door. "I know you need your time to cope, to grieve, but when you get yourself together, remember there's a wonderful woman out there who needs you."

I lay on the couch knowing she couldn't see me anymore and let silent tears fall. One side of me ached for what I'd experienced, the other ached for what Jade had lived through.

Chapter 26

I eventually went back to work when I found that numb place where you hide when everything around is nothing but pain. Miranda came in daily, but she didn't spend as much time as she used to. I wasn't a joy to be around, but that wasn't the only reason. She was spending her time with Jade, too. Miranda was like an extension of me. It comforted and shamed me knowing that she was doing what I should've and wouldn't.

But it wasn't Miranda who jerked me out of my well of self-pity, it was Deb. She showed up one evening as I was about to lock down the store. I hadn't seen her since our quasi-intervention, and I figured she was there to exact revenge. She walked in wordlessly, and I locked the door behind her. "You want to come back to the house, have a drink?" I asked.

"Yeah," she said with a nod.

I poured us both a glass of wine. We sat at the kitchen table. I think we were waiting for the other to speak first. She grew tired of the game. "Self-pity is a motherfucker, isn't it?" I looked at her, wondering if she was talking about herself or me. Deb straightened and looked at me chin up. "I'm in therapy. My first few sessions were about forgiveness. Forgiving you and Angel, Miranda—myself." Her dark eyes narrowed. "I'm not there yet, but I'm learning."

"That's great."

"You can learn, too," she said coolly. "It's been over a week. You've had your time to cope. Now it's time for action."

I still didn't know what she was talking about. "I'm sorry if I hurt you—"

"I'm not talking about myself. I'm talking about Jade."

Anger swept over me like a wildfire. "Did Miranda tell you?"

"No, Jade did." Deb's eyes were hard. "With Jade's permission, Miranda invited me over. Though I haven't experienced what Jade has, I'm struggling with my own issues. We commiserated, and at least for me, it was very liberating." She leaned in close enough for me to feel her breath on my face. "Sometimes, you have to realize you're not the only one with a problem."

Excuses ran through my brain and pushed at my clamped lips. *I can handle this myself. I don't need help. Leave me alone and let me cope with this in my own way.* But I couldn't say that to Deb because she'd already said the same things, and I knew she'd throw it all back in my face as invalid, as I had done to her. I sat mute.

"I'm learning to accept that I'm a survivor, but Jade? She's in a class all her own. I'm surrounded by friends, a loving partner. Jade's done it on her own." Deb slammed her hand on the table when I looked away. "Don't you fucking dare dismiss that with a shake of your head, Sloan. She's a remarkable woman who deserves a hell of a lot more than what you've given her." She pointed a shaking finger in my face. "You're angry, Miranda warned me about that, and I can see it all over you. You have a right to be furious with her parents, but not with her."

I knew the excuse was poor as it came out of my mouth, but it was all I had. "How could she sit back and let them get away with it? How come she hasn't filed charges? Her father could very well be doing this to some other kid." My voice broke. "How come she's not angry anymore?"

Deb was a tough customer. She wasn't going to be softened by a show of emotion. "Don't be an idiot. You know after all these years that it would be very difficult for her to prove what happened. Would you want to be put on the stand and testify if it got that far? To look into impassionate faces and tell about the worst time of your life and hoped that they believed?" She pointed in my face again. "*You* don't have to answer that because we both know you're a coward."

I gritted my teeth, and I knew my face showed murderous

rage, but Deb was not backing down. "You wanted time to cope with this in your own way, and it's been given to you. How dare you demand that Jade react the way you think she should! How dare you judge her!"

Deb could've backhanded me, and it wouldn't have hurt half as much as the truth. All my anger and hostility dissolved into the hurt I'd kept buried beneath hot embers of hate. I released it in a howl as I cried, letting the agony flow like lava. And Deb was there pulling me into her arms and rocking me for what seemed like the entire night.

"You're scared," Deb said later when I had calmed. We were sitting on the kitchen floor leaning against the wall.

My voice was hoarse. "I have finally lost my heart, and there's this to deal with. I don't know if I'm strong enough."

Deb reached up and pulled my glass from the table. "Drink," she said as she got her own. I sipped at the wine and winced as it burned my raw throat. "None of us is strong enough alone." She shook her head and laughed. "I hate that I need help, but I need you and Angel and fucking Miranda, too." She poked me in the leg. "You need us, too, and so does Jade."

"I have no idea how to fix this."

"You don't. Time and love will heal all, or so I'm told. Jade needs to see you cry, and you need to let her." Deb took a long swallow from her glass. "She's losing faith in you, Sloan. This is a woman that has pulled herself up by her own bootstraps many a time. Your silence equals rejection to her, and she's preparing to move on."

Chapter 27

I waited in the parking lot for Jade to leave work. I had no idea what to say. I just wanted to pull her into my arms and beg for forgiveness. My heart pounded in my chest as thunder rolled overhead and the door to the gym opened. I had my hand on the car door handle when I saw Jade and Jacquelyn emerge together. Jacquelyn was smiling and talking. Jade's face looked like stone. My fingers lost their grip on the handle when Jade passed her truck and got into Jacquelyn's Infinity.

I watched the car as it rolled past. Jade in the passenger's seat was looking the opposite way out the window. Closest to me was Jacquelyn, who looked positively giddy. I sank down in my seat and pinched the bridge of my nose. I knew what Jade was doing. I had done it so many times myself. For a while, she'd lose herself in the arms of a woman to escape her existence for a time. The solace found there would be short-lived, and in the morning light, she would feel even more hollow than the night before.

I left a spray of gravel as I pulled onto the highway. The Mustang zoomed under my command. They had a lead on me, and I broke every speed limit to make up for the lost time. I had a vague idea of where Jacquelyn lived, but I didn't know which house. When I pulled off of Highway 98, I could just make out the Infinity's taillights before it disappeared into a curve. Jacquelyn wasn't wasting any time.

A car pulled onto the road ahead of me. I couldn't pass as two more were coming toward me in the oncoming lane. When it was clear, I punched the gas pedal, and the Mustang answered my request. I put the tach in the red as I shifted gears, cursing that I'd lost sight of the Infinity. I turned off the road onto a street with a thirty-five-mile-an-hour speed limit and dropped to forty-five as I looked for the white car. I found it and skidded into the drive. Jacquelyn and Jade paused at the first landing of stairs when I pulled behind the Infinity.

I had no rehearsed speech. I had no idea what to say, but my heart did, and I gave her full authority. Jade was looking at me in the muted light. I could feel her stare, but it was Jacquelyn who asked the obvious question. "Why are you here?"

"Jade." I gripped the railing and watched as she tilted her head back to let the steady rain soak her face. "I'm so sorry."

"Go home," Jacquelyn said. "This is private property and—"

I glared at Jacquelyn. "I know who waits for you up there." The light from the porch shone down on me like a spotlight on a stage. "I know who you are, and I know what you do. If you want your precious secret kept, then quietly go up the stairs and close the door."

Jacquelyn stared at me for a minute. I couldn't see her features, but I knew her face registered surprise. She took one look at Jade, who was still staring up at the heavens, and walked away.

I walked up two steps out of the light. "Jade, I know at times you felt unworthy of me, unworthy of love, but you never knew how unworthy of you I felt, still feel. I've never met anyone more extraordinary, and I know I never will." She didn't look at me; instead, she held her face up to the rain and continued to let it wash her face. "I did exactly what I said I would never do, I let you down."

Jade didn't move, nor did she speak. I wiped at my face angrily as tears mixed with the falling rain. "I didn't willingly go into your mind. I thought I was asleep. But I saw—and God help us both—I felt what you went through. I know you intended to tell me in your own time, and you'll probably resent this, but I'm fairly certain I wouldn't have grasped the gravity of it all if I hadn't lived it." I swallowed back the lump of emotion clogging my throat. I never knew what strength and courage really were until then. I clutched my chest as the realization dawned on me. "I'm not worthy of you, Jade. I want you, need you…love you, but…"

I hung my head in shame. "I failed you. I'm so sorry."

Suddenly, I felt like I was lifting one side of a very heavy box, the weight was too much for me to bear alone. Reluctantly, I felt it slipping from my hands and turned to go. I exhaled loudly as the rain began to pour. "I'll give you a ride back to the gym if you want." I turned and walked to my car, my hand felt numb as I reached for the handle. Something gripped my other, and I turned to see Jade.

Without a word, she took my hand and put it to her chest. Her eyes implored me to take that one last secret. I felt forgiveness, hope, and most of all, love.

"Will you take me…home?"

Had she not been touching me, I would've misunderstood. She wasn't asking for a ride to her apartment or even to my house; she was asking for forever. "Yes, I'll take you, and I'll never let you go again."

Epilogue

"Look at this." Miranda pointed at the TV with the remote. The music outside drowned out what the reporter was saying, but I didn't need to hear it to know what happened. A picture of Senator Priest was on the screen, and next to it was a still shot of Jacquelyn climbing into her car surrounded by the media. She had cashed in.

The party was in full swing. The guests of honor, Lonna and Paige, were beaming. I watched them through the kitchen window as I sipped a drink. There was more than one kind of love affair, and I guess at times we all take them for granted when something new comes along.

There's a love affair between parent and child, the sweetness of loving and caring for a little one and watching them grow into adulthood. Not being a parent, I had no reference, but I had known the love of a woman who had not given birth to me. I adored and respected her. She was my safety, my rock.

And there's the love affair between friends. I'd been blessed with that, too. We bickered and fought, we loved and lost together, but the affection that remained among us was a beauty of its own.

And then, there is the romantic love affair that makes the heart soar and plummet, but that ride is the most exciting of all.

I looked over at Marty as she peeled a shrimp and popped it into Jade's mouth. Jade looked up at me then as she chewed, and I felt like my heart was too big for my chest. The love I felt swelled within me, and I couldn't help but smile.

Our ride into the sunset wasn't an easy one. We talked about a lot of painful, hurtful things, then we put it behind us. I knew all her secrets and she mine, but I didn't know Jade. Each day was a new discovery, some good, some…not so good. I'm sure she could say the same of me. A bond formed between us, though, and when the dark dreams of night came, we clung together until the sun arose and we began a new day—together.

I didn't need to pry into her mind to know that another could never take my place.

About the Author

Robin Alexander is the author of the Goldie Award-winning *Gloria's Secret* and eight other novels for Intaglio Publications—*Gloria's Inn, Gift of Time, Murky Waters, The Taking of Eden, Love's Someday, Pitifully Ugly, Undeniable,* and *A Devil in Disguise.* Her short story "Crossing the Line" can be found in the anthology *Romance for Life.*

Robin spends her days working with the staff of Intaglio and her nights with her own writings. She still manages to find time to spend with her partner, Becky, and their three dogs and four cats.

You can reach her at robinalex65@yahoo.com. You can also visit her Web site at www.robinalexanderbooks.com.

You May Also Enjoy

Undeniable
by Robin Alexander
ISBN: 978-1-935216-28-5

After twenty years, Samantha Jackson comes face to face with Jennifer Tanner at a memorial service for a mutual friend. Her plan is simple—pay her respects and maybe have an amicable conversation with the one person who affected her life the most.

Jennifer needs answers to questions that she has carried into adulthood. Circumstances, though unfortunate, have given her that opportunity. She wanted closure; instead, the revelations leave her with anything but resolution.

Two souls come to realize that sometimes love is simply—undeniable.

A Devil In Disguise
by Robin Alexander
ISBN: 978-1-935216-26-1

After suffering a life-changing accident, Natalie Simmons is ready to begin living again. Two distinctly different women enter her life, and she finds herself drawn to both. A choice has to be made. Will she pick the right one or unknowingly choose the devil in disguise?

Pitifully Ugly
By Robin Alexander
ISBN: 978-1-935216-21-6

Hot, sweet, sexy and funny.

Shannon Brycen believes she is the epitome of pitifully ugly.

Kalen, Shannon's overly social sister, is determined to play match-maker and find a special someone for her sister.

After a disastrous date with one of Kalen's recent selections, Shannon decides to take her love life back into her own hands by joining the local lesbian cyber match-maker.

Mid thirties, still single, house broken but rabid. If you're looking for something different then I'm your girl. Write me if you dare...P.U.

Maybe it wasn't the best idea to build her profile after consuming half a bottle of her favorite wine...or to use a picture of herself at the age of six - after she had cut her own hair-as her online profile photograph.

Hiding behind the online persona of *Pitifully Ugly*, Shannon finds the courage to meet new women and face the disaster called dating. As her charming personality surfaces, Shannon's search for the perfect match may be closer than she realizes.

Published by
Intaglio Publications
Walker, La.
You can purchase other Intaglio
Publications books online at
www.lgbtbookshop.com/
or at
your local bookstore.

Visit us on the web and read excerpts from
upcoming novels
www.intagliopub.com